# THE BADMEN

Center Point
Large Print

Also by Bill Brooks and available from Center Point Large Print:

*A Bullet for Billy*
*The Horses*

# THE
# BADMEN

## Bill Brooks

CENTER POINT LARGE PRINT
THORNDIKE, MAINE

This Center Point Large Print edition is published
in the year 2014 by arrangement with
Golden West Literary Agency.

The text of this Large Print edition is unabridged.
In other aspects, this book may vary
from the original edition.
Printed in the United States of America
on permanent paper.
Set in 16-point Times New Roman type.

ISBN: 978-1-62899-150-5

Library of Congress Cataloging-in-Publication Data

Brooks, Bill, 1943–
The badmen / Bill Brooks. — Center Point Large Print edition.
pages ; cm.
Summary: "Able Guthrie rides out to rescue his former wife after she is
abducted by a bank robber and taken into the Badlands"
—Provided by publisher.
ISBN 978-1-62899-150-5 (library binding : alk. paper)
1. Large type books. I. Title.
PS3552.R65863B3 2014
813′.54—dc23
                                                                2014011845

To Diane and Walt,
who know about love, friendship,
and sharing their lives with old writers.
And to my children:
Joshua, Jason, Kurt, and Tricia.

# CHAPTER 1

## Texas Panhandle, 1876

He rode in looking for Charley Justice.

For the last three days he had ridden across land so flat and sparse that the only things he saw were coyotes, cactus, and cattle. The wind blew hard as hell and all the time. Cloudless days of sun almost fried him, and clear cold nights froze his limbs. It was a land that seemed intent on keeping out strangers.

The town was called Brother, and the only good thing Guthrie could see in it was a tough little building that had Whiskey & Beer painted on its front. It looked like the only place in town to buy some liquid comfort and maybe some information. There were a half a dozen wood structures along the one and only street. They reminded him of old men leaning into the wind—gray, sagging buildings that looked as though they could use a rest.

Dry, brittle balls of tumbleweeds rolled and bounced along the street pushed by the wind, some stopping against buildings, others continuing on in a seemingly endless journey to nowhere.

It did not escape Guthrie's attention as he tied his mount in front of the saloon that there was no activity on the streets. The sky had scudded gray and damned if it did not feel like snow.

Habit made him unflap the lower half of his sheepskin coat and adjust the .41-caliber Colt strapped to his hip before he entered the whiskey parlor.

Once inside, he waited by the doors until his eyes could adjust. When they had, he scanned the knot of unfriendly faces. Charley Justice was not among them.

Eyes, squeezed narrow from being exposed too long to sun and wind, surveyed his presence before returning to what they had been watching. He returned the patrons' interest with equal measure. These were common cowtown men: ranchers, drifters, maybe even a rustler or two if the truth were known.

It wasn't thirst so much as it was the need to kill the pain in his hip that made Guthrie order a whiskey. The man behind the bar asked him if he had a dollar to pay for it before pouring.

"A powerful price for drinking liquor, isn't it?" questioned Guthrie.

"We don't get whiskey through here every day," growled the barkeeper. "You don't have to drink it—you could ride to Ulvade, it ain't but a two-day ride from here." The barkeep's smile was sour and crooked.

Guthrie let the man know with an unflinching stare that he did not approve of the gouging, but put a silver dollar on the bar anyway. The man swept it up in his hand and poured the drink.

Guthrie took it to a far corner—a place where he could watch the door well enough. He pulled out a busted-back chair from the table and sat down. He pulled the Colt out and laid it on the table in front of him and put glass to his lips with his left hand. The liquor stung his wind-cracked lips but warmed his mouth and his insides.

The place smelled of smoke and men who didn't bathe much. What little conversation there was, was spoken in low, harsh tones. More noise was made by boots scraping chair rungs, and coughing and belching.

He sipped the whiskey slow. Because it hurt and because it was a dollar a glass. He pulled a railroader's watch from his coat pocket and checked the time. He'd wait one more hour for Justice to show.

He had been tracking the man for nearly three months, and as far as he could figure, this was where he should meet up with him. *They say a bird always returns to his nest.* And this strip of the Panhandle sure was Charley Justice's nest, he had kin all up and down it.

Guthrie tried to ignore the pain in his hip. But

sometimes, like now, it had a way of working its way up into his mind to where he could not deny it. When it got bad like it was now, it caused him to remember all over again how the Reb had shot him out of the saddle two entire days after the battle of Gettysburg was finished.

He remembered how peaceful it had been riding down the road, in column, with his cavalry command. He remembered how the sun fell through the trees and dappled the road in front of him, and how mild the weather had turned after being hellfire hot during the battle itself.

It was true, as far as he was concerned, that the shot that hits you is the one you never hear. It stung like a hammered nail and his whole leg went numb. And suddenly, he could no longer keep his balance in the saddle and the ache turned into a small fire. The mean part was, they never caught the Reb sharpshooter who did it.

The army surgeon ran a "silk handkerchief" through the wound and cauterized it until Guthrie could smell his own flesh frying.

"You got lucky, soldier," the surgeon had told him. "Just knocked off a piece of hip bone and put two little tear holes in you. Another couple of inches lower and it would've taken off your oysters." He chuckled.

"I've known men who were funny and you're not one of them," he snapped.

The doctor sewed him up with a line thick enough to string catfish on and left him to his misery.

Coldness and sitting too long made Guthrie remember just how damn sorry that war had been for him.

The rattling of the saloon doors and a cold blast of air broke his reverie. Silhouetted in a frame of pearly light was the man he had come for.

Someone yelled, "Shut the damn door!" and the big man tossed an angry look in the direction of the carper. He kicked the door shut behind him and shook a dusting of snow from the faded serape draped over his shoulders. His battered, flat-brimmed hat was tied on by a blue scarf knotted under his bearded chin. Wet strands of tangled hair gathered around his face, and his mustache and beard still held drops of ice. Guthrie judged him to be a plate of beans short of three hundred pounds.

Justice took in what he could see of the place before moving to the bar. His misfortune was he did not see the stranger in the sheepskin coat sitting in the far corner. Guthrie's fortune was that Charley Justice had eyes no better than a wild hog's.

Guthrie studied the big man who moved to the bar and laid the heavy, long gun down on the board in front of him. Justice ordered a bucket of beer and stared at it a long, full minute. Guthrie could only guess what was under the Mexican blanket Justice wore.

Clearly, Justice was a man to be reckoned with—just standing there, he seemed full of danger. Guthrie sat patiently waiting to see if Cora Nevers would show. The trail had been long and hard, and he wanted to take them both back to stand trial for the killing of the judge.

Judge Hays Nevers had retired from the bench the year previous, and right after, had taken up with Cora—a parlor girl who was long on looks, but short on heart. Loneliness and age had turned the once sharp-minded judge to a man with clouded reason. Nevers himself knew that. Right after the marriage, in fact, he had confided to Guthrie that maybe he had made a mistake in marrying the girl. The judge had said that his own kids had been against his marrying a woman with such a shady past, but the old man did not want to admit publicly that his wife was too young and wild for him.

He confided to Guthrie that, in spite of everything, he loved her. "Cora is like fire in my blood."

Guthrie was a man to understand what being in love could do to a man's mind. He sympathized with his old friend, but felt plain helpless to offer him advice on the matter.

Three months ago, the old man was found shot to death in his bed. Cora and many of her good clothes were missing. Someone noted she had been back to her old haunts the night previous, and had been seen with a fellow named Charley Justice. By the time the judge's body was found, Justice had disappeared too.

The family had put up a reward of twelve hundred dollars for the pair of them. Sheriff Hobe Waters appealed to his old friend Able Guthrie to strike the trail after them.

"I did find out from those who heard him bragging while he was doing his carousing," said Waters to Guthrie in his appeal, "that he's from down in the Texas Panhandle. My jurisdiction doesn't go that far, and even if it did, my going after him would leave this town without any law whatsoever."

Guthrie did not feel inclined to take up the chase, even though he felt terrible about the fate of his old friend.

Waters knew Guthrie had been planning to leave the territory for Arizona long before the incident of Judge Nevers's murder. "The money put up by the family could help you buy that spread you've been bending my ear about."

"It's not the money, Hobe," he had told the sheriff. "He was a friend, but I just don't feel I have it in me anymore to run down outlaws. Why not hand the case over to the U.S. marshals?"

"I already did that. Do you think they'll put this case ahead of all others they've got just because the judge was a friend of ours? Hell, they may never catch up with Justice if he's left the territory—which I am damn sure he has." Hobe had kicked over a chair in his disgust and frustration. "Able, what the hell is wrong with getting rewarded for doing the right thing? You could use that money to get your dream down there in Arizona. There's not one damn thing wrong with that. . . ."

"Okay. I'll go after him. Just let up on the speeches!" Guthrie remembered that first day on the trail wondering why, after an all-day saddle sore, he had given in to the prodding of Hobe Waters. But he knew the reason plain enough: *Because he was an old friend, and because the judge had been an old friend. A man did not just walk away from old friends.*

Now he had found the man. Maybe the woman was somewhere around too. Guthrie figured that it had to have been Justice who pulled the trigger on the judge, so even if he never caught the woman, he'd at least take this one back.

Justice held the pail of beer in one hand and slowly turned his attention to the rest of the room. Guthrie watched the man's Adam's apple bob with each swallow of beer.

He decided he had waited long enough. It was obvious that the woman was not going to show. He pulled the warrant from his coat pocket, held it aloft, and said, "You'd be Charley Justice, judging from the size of you."

The big man's piggish eyes searched the dimness of the room, his right hand moved toward the long gun on the bar.

"You take hold of that saddle gun, I'll be forced to shoot you where you stand!" said Guthrie.

Justice zeroed in on the commanding voice from somewhere in the far corner—he still could not make out the man's face. He gauged the distance, his mind stepping off the space between them. The hard press of the hand ax he carried beneath the serape brought him some measure of comfort.

"You'd have to be some shot at this distance!" bellowed the big man.

"Man your size, wouldn't take much skill, I'd say."

"What is it you want of me, mister?" asked Justice, trying his best to recognize the challenger. "I do you some harm somewheres along the road, have I?"

"Not me, but a friend."

"You the law?"

"Of a sort."

"What sort?"

"Well, I got a warrant for your arrest, and I got this-here Colt. I'd say that makes it official."

"Arrest for what?"

"The murder of Judge Hays Nevers."

"That man was kilt in the Black Hills—this ain't the Black Hills! This is Texas!"

15

"Where's Cora Nevers?"

"Who?"

"The woman that helped you do the old man in? Where's she at?"

Justice gave a grunt and then grinned a dark, stained smile that lifted high the thick mustaches. "Hell, I sold her out to a whorehouse down in Tascosa—she wasn't all that much of a gal, anyways. Kinda trash-mouthed. She had a mean streak in her I couldn't tolerate. Hell, mister. You lookin' for that old man's killer—it'd be her. Me, I wouldn't hurt a flea if it was to crawl all the way through my hair."

"Like hell."

# CHAPTER 2

Guthrie could no longer contain his anger at the man's insolence and manner. He did not know Cora Nevers except by name, but he knew a killer when he saw one, and Justice fit the bill.

"I have all but run out of talk," he said. "You've had your say, let's finish this business."

"Look here, friend. I've got family all up and down these parts. You think we're just goin' to ride along safe as preachers, you stickin' a gun up my backside, with nobody doin' a thing to stop it?" Justice seemed too sure of himself to suit Guthrie.

"Anybody comes crawling out of the wood-work to try and save your sorry hide would make it hard on all of us. But it would be harder on you first!"

"Easy now, mister. If it's money that could change your thinkin'—hell, I've got plenty I can get for you—dust, silver, paper, you name it. What's say we palaver over it? There ain't any use to either one of us letting this be our last day on earth!"

"I don't take my business lightly," said Guthrie,

pulling a pair of iron handcuffs from his outside coat pocket. He tossed them and they clattered to a stop near the big man's boots.

"You put those on and then finish your beer and we'll be on our way."

Justice eyed the handcuffs like they were snakes lying at his feet. Guthrie had just begun to slide the Colt back into his holster when the big man made his move.

He moved lightning quick for a man his size. Guthrie was caught off guard—his own confidence had gotten in his way.

Guthrie's first shot splintered the bar inches from where Justice had been standing. The man was a blur bearing down on him, the hand ax raised above his head.

Guthrie's second shot kicked up dust high on the big man's shoulder and knocked him half sideways, and he screamed, "Goddamn," and twisted himself back around in less time than a deep breath. The quick burst of gunfire made the bystanders hug the floor.

Justice had closed the distance between him and Guthrie to where they could spit on each other. The big man was lunging toward Guthrie when the Colt banged again. Guthrie had aimed the shot at the belt buckle of the enraged man. But in so doing, he had taken a step backward and tangled up in the legs of the busted-back chair he had been sitting in and threw off his aim.

The shot shattered Justice's left kneecap. He screamed in pain as he crashed to the floor, holding onto his leg like it might fly away.

"You shot my damn leg bone in two!" he cried through clenched teeth. "I'm a sum-a-bitch you didn't go and ruin me good."

A cloud of acrid blue smoke hung in the air like a small storm cloud that had no place to go. Guthrie felt a sense of relief wash over him—he hadn't hit a damn thing he had aimed at. It just as easily could have been him lying there on the floor with a hatchet buried in his skull.

Guthrie felt no sympathy for the man. He knocked out the spent shells and they clattered on the floor while he reloaded and then holstered the Colt.

"Ain't you at least goin' to call a doctor, or sumpthin'?" he pleaded with Guthrie. "This leg's all on fire!"

Guthrie looked about him. Somewhere right after the last shot, a crowd had gathered in the saloon.

"Is there a doc in this town?" he asked, speaking to no one in particular. Someone volunteered that there was, but that he didn't treat free.

Guthrie looked at the man keenly. "You care to say how much he'd charge for something like this?"

The talker peered over the shoulder of the man

19

in front of him to get a better look at the victim.

"I'd say ten dollars, at least."

"Well, since you know so damn much about all of this, you mind carrying yourself on over to the doc's place and getting him to handle this—I got ten dollars if he don't," said Guthrie pointing down at Justice, who seemed to be losing his color.

"Don't have to run, I'm him," said the talker. "Some of you boys help this poor soul to get over to my place, will ya."

Justice let out another squawk as several men lifted him to his feet and he tried bearing down on the shot leg.

"That leg's going to pain you something awful on the ride back to Deadwood," Guthrie told him. "And even after it heals, it's going to gnaw on you like a dog chewing every time it gets too cold, or you sit too long."

"For a man what looks like he should be retired on a porch somewhere, you sure got a mean streak in you!" said the hobbled man.

Able Guthrie ignored the remark as several men felt what it was like to carry three hundred pounds of wounded man.

Three months of searching and the tension of the fight had left him dog tired. While Justice was being patched up Guthrie inquired after a room and was told there was a boardinghouse down at the end of the street. He stepped out into the cold air. It had quit snowing but the wind still cut. The street was quiet and the cold mud sucked at his boots and clear to the other end of the street seemed a long way to walk for a man nearly forty with an aching hip.

# CHAPTER 3

## Deadwood, May 1876

Guthrie rode the big chestnut gelding down the narrow, muddy street. He held the reins of the swaybacked bay that looked as though she might collapse under the weight of Charley Justice, whose left leg was wrapped in a dirty bandage and stuck out stiff as a board.

The street was jammed with wagons and teamsters carrying lumber, casks of nails, tools, mining equipment. There were boards piled up in places waiting to be built into something. Grim-faced men lounged in ill-fitting clothes and women in gingham dresses and bonnets the size of pillows shuttled down what board sidewalks there were. There were other men in derbies and tailored suits who surveyed everything in sight.

The buildings were cheek by jowl, both sides of the street. Every nature of business could be found: Black Hills Restaurant; Bob's Butcher Shop & Groceries; L. B. & Son—Gunsmith; The Republic Club; Dr. Fine—Dentistry; Deadwood Drugstore Featuring Doc Hostetter's Stomach

Bitters; J. Engle's Barbershop; Wallace & Barns: Attorneys & Real Estate Agents.

And for the gamier side of life, one just had to walk to the end of town—either direction—to find the whiskey tents and crib houses. And if crib whores were not what a fellow was looking for, a little farther walk, or a short buggy ride brought a body to D. W. Conner's Hog Farm, complete with red velvet draperies and corn-husk mattresses in each of twelve rooms.

Charley Justice, sullen as he was, couldn't help but feel the longing to wallow in the worst that Deadwood had to offer. Able Guthrie remembered why he longed for that place down on the Little Colorado in Arizona Territory. Being back in Deadwood also caused him to remember a sorry part of his life. He had purposely avoided going by her place on the way in. She was another reason he had to get shed of the place as soon as he settled up with the sheriff.

He reined in, in front of a plain building that leaned up against Tuttle's Tents store on the one side and Caleb Joregeson's Mining and Prospecting Equipment store on the other. The sign over the door said Sheriff. He tied the reins of both horses to the hitch rail and stepped up on the boardwalk.

He didn't bother to knock.

Hobe Waters was testing the strength of a pot of coffee he was boiling atop a potbellied stove—

he used a rag to lift off the lid. He turned half-way around at Able's unexpected entrance. He gingerly dropped the lid back on the pot and greeted his old friend with a warm handshake. Looking over Able's shoulder, and through the smudged window, he could see a crowd gathering around the forlorn prisoner. "I see you didn't have to bring him back in a meat wagon," he commented.

"No, I had to shoot him twice just to bring him this far, though," said the gaunt detective.

"Well, it wouldn't have been any loss to the territory to have brought him in face down," said Hobe Waters, staring at the bulk of man on the horse outside.

"I wasn't able to find the woman," said Guthrie. "Justice said he sold her down in Tascosa, but the chances she's still there are slim. I figured he was the one that killed the judge, anyway. She probably didn't weep any tears over the matter, but she probably didn't do the killing herself."

"You're most likely right—it'd be hard to get a jury to convict a woman, anyway. Did he say why they did it?"

"He and I didn't hold much conversation on the way back. What little he did say had to do mostly with the condition of his wounds."

"I suspect it was robbery," said Hobe. "That tends to be all the motivation most trash needs these days. It seems like such a waste."

"It always is," said Guthrie. "Is that coffee ready yet?"

Hobe poured out a cup and Able blew the steam off before putting the coffee to his lips.

"You reckon you could get some men to help Justice out of the saddle?" asked Able. "My back is total wore out from helping him down and up again all this trip back."

"Tooly! Get yourself out here, I need you to do a chore," hollered Hobe back to where the cells were. Tooly was a busted-down drunk who Hobe locked up more for his sake than for that of the town's. In exchange for the room and board, Tooly ran errands for Hobe and was an extra pair of ears around town.

Tooly came out of the back looking as though he had awakened from the dead. Guthrie had seen consumption victims who looked better. Hobe told the floater to go enlist some help to bring the prisoner inside and lock him up in one of the cells—which one didn't matter—they were all empty at the moment.

"Not mine!" pleaded Tooly. "Man might have nits."

"Any one but yours," said Hobe. Tooly eyed the two men, then left.

Hobe studied his old friend in that moment of silence while Able sipped the hot brew and watched half aimlessly the activity through the window. It seemed to Hobe that Guthrie had aged a couple of years rather than the few months since he had left Deadwood. Able had removed his brown Stetson revealing streaks of white in the sandy-colored hair. Hobe also took note that the pinched places around the corners of the clear gray eyes seemed more creased. Maybe the eyes had seen too much in the detective's forty years. Hobe thought it was more than just coincidence that Able's face seemed chiseled and flinty, the same way the wind and rain chisel mountain rock. Men who lived in the places Able had lived most of his life had faces like that.

Many men Able's age had gone to flab, but Guthrie was as lean and rawhidy as a mustang. Unlike most men of the time, Able did keep his blond mustache trimmed neat and short—it was a matter of personal pride.

"Curly Bill Cook is in town," Hobe said casually. Able turned from staring out the window—several men were struggling to get Charley Justice off his horse. "Came in yesterday, him and Texas Jack. They pitched a tent and Bill has taken up office at Nutall & Mann's Saloon."

"How does he seem?"

"You know Bill," said Hobe, his mouth pressed into a slight smile. "All fancy dressed in a black suit and a boiled shirt. He's wearing sixty-dollar boots."

Guthrie remembered when Bill was a lot less of a dude than he had heard tell he had become lately. Bill was a handsome man though, even in buckskins.

"One thing, though," added Hobe. "He seems old. Not so much the way he looks, it's the way he moves. Rumor has it that his eyes have gotten bad but that he's too damn vain to wear specs. I sure hope to hell no young tough decides to take him on. I'm not sure Bill could stand the challenge."

"I wouldn't worry on it too hard," remarked Able. "Bad eyes and slow, I bet he's still a caution. I wouldn't want to be the one to present him trouble."

It had been a long time since the three of them had all gathered in one place at the same time. In fact, as Able recalled it, it had been down in Abilene, Kansas, five years previous when Bill was appointed town constable after One-eyed Fred Williams got his head chopped off trying to serve a warrant on a farmer.

Back then, it was an uncommon night when the three of them didn't gather around a table in the saloon and do a little serious gambling. Truth was Hobe was the best at cards, while Bill was pretty terrible. But cards was just a part of wild nights back in Abilene. There was the drinking— and the women. Curly Bill Cook, Hobe Waters, and Able Guthrie were the cocks that crowed the loudest.

But it didn't last—nothing ever did—and come

that December, Bill got canned, Hobe went north, and Able went farther west.

Hobe was a deputy under Newt Fellows, who mostly shuffled papers, played keno, and succumbed to the charms of soiled doves; Hobe did all the real law enforcement. Hobe didn't mind. Newt passed away one night in the arms of a crib girl named Bucktooth Minnie. The mourners included Newt's wife and five children. Hobe was given the job of sheriff, and that's the way it stood the day Able Guthrie came riding in to Deadwood.

That was a year ago.

"I work at whatever is legal and don't have to be done on foot," he told Hobe that spring day. Hobe offered him a deputy's job. Able declined. "I appreciate your offering," he told Hobe. "But truth is, I hold special the idea of choosing what I will or will not do. A man gets my age, it gets real important to be independent—I'm not exactly sure why—it just does."

After a while, however, Hobe realized that Able hadn't chosen to base his activity out of Deadwood purely by happenstance. Tooly had let the cat out of the bag one day while he was hanging out the jail-cell mattresses to air.

"I heard tell your pal Guthrie's been sporting around with Ben Matters's missus," he said casual as spring rain to Hobe.

"Foolish talk like that could get you dusted," said Hobe, irritated by such gossip.

"I heard tell, too, that the reason is, she used to be married to that-there detective long before she married our bank president."

"Tooly, you hang out those mattresses and beat the dust out of them, and keep your trap shut, or the next time you fall down drunk in the street, I'll leave you there!"

The man scuttled out of the room with a mattress draped over his shoulder and did not return the rest of the day. But it did not stop the concern that he had built in the sheriff's head. He knew that Able had been married some time ago, for Able had let it slip in conversation one night when the whiskey had made him maudlin. But Able never mentioned who she was or what had happened. He now hoped to hell it wasn't true what Tooly had told him. Over the next few months, he found out it was.

"You know," Able said suddenly, "I have been thinking that as soon as I collect for the capture of Justice, I'm going to that place down in Arizona down on the Little Colorado. Good country down there . . . warm most of the time. Maybe I can dry this sore hip of mine out enough to keep me out of an invalid chair before I turn fifty."

"I'd say that would be a damn pleasant thing for you to do," replied Hobe. "Maybe I could come visit sometime."

"Hell, why not," said Able.

"You want to go see Bill?" asked Hobe.

"I had planned on it. I want to soak in a hot tub of soapy water first and feel what clean clothes are like. What say I meet up with you here in a couple of hours and we'll walk over together."

"It would be a pleasure."

"Then say six o'clock it is," said Able, glancing at the watch he pulled from his coat pocket. "I'm heading over to Nettie Longren's boarding-house."

The two men shook hands and Guthrie stepped outside. Several men were still struggling with a cussing Charley Justice. "Goddamn it all to hell," he yelled at them. "Might as well shoot me in my other leg for all the pain yore puttin' on me!"

"Wal, if you wasn't such a big tub of lard, you wouldn't need no help!" yelled one of the frustrated group.

The insult caused Charley Justice to whomp down on the head of the nearest of the lot that was tussling with him. A general struggle ensued and Justice came tumbling out of the saddle atop the would-be assistants. Able stepped around them as they struggled desperately to untangle themselves from the flailing desperado.

A woman with iron-gray hair who looked as though she had pillows stuffed under her dress answered Able's knock at the door. As soon as she saw him, her looks softened a bit and she began chiding him over his absence. She made him sit in the parlor and have tea and sorghum cookies with her, "like a civilized man would do."

"Your room's nearly ready," she told him, "as soon as Lucy changes the bedding. We had it rented to two Texans. They left this morning. You know how Texas men can be about their personal habits," she confided in a polite whisper. "I just want to make sure you don't pick up anything unwanted from them." And as though to justify it all, she added: "But what's a body supposed to do? You just can't not rent to somebody because they might have lice—I'd have to turn away half the business I do if that were the case."

Able said he understood and wondered if he might take a few of the cookies up to his room for later. She knew he was just being polite, and she admired him for it. And for being good company to her. It wasn't often a woman her age got to keep company with a fine man such as Able Guthrie.

# CHAPTER 4

Hobe Waters was coming up the sidewalk, the ring of his spurs matching each step. Able had just finished a long, hot bath next door to Nettie's at Sam Chin's Bath House and put on a fresh set of clothes.

"I decided to swing by and pick you up," he said just as Able was coming out the door. "You look like a twenty-dollar whore on a Saturday night, spruced up as you are." Able was wearing clean denims, blue shirt, and his brown Stetson, now brushed and cleaned as well. Nettie had even taken care to see that his boots were rubbed and polished. Feeling self-conscious over Hobe's remark, Able stroked the smooth places of his face and coughed.

Able suggested they walk over to Nutall's in hopes of running into Curly Bill. It was getting on late in the afternoon and much of the earlier day's activity had slowed down to where it almost seemed pleasant. For both of them, it felt familiar and comfortable to be strolling down the walk side by side, hearing the clomp of their boots on the boards, touching the brims of their hats to passing ladies.

Nutall & Mann's was crowded and smoky and the light was poor. Men stood around in groups, sat at tables and at the bar. They talked loud and cussed and laughed and played cards.

Able and Hobe squeezed in at the bar and waited patiently to order from one of the two barkeeps who were busy pulling the porcelain handles of beer dispensers and pouring whiskey into glasses. Nobody seemed to mind much. They used the time to scan the room for their famous friend. Able spotted a table with an inordinate number of men standing around it. "I'd say that's where Bill's sitting," he said to Hobe, nodding in the direction of the knot of men.

"He still draws a lot of interest," remarked Able. "All those dime novels made him legendary."

"They say the syphilis is making him go blind," said Hobe.

"If true, I'd hate to be around if someone calls him out. Bad eyes don't cause the hands to go slow, but sure makes hitting what you're aiming at something special."

Hobe laughed and said, "I think maybe we ought not to just walk up and yell 'surprise,' huh?"

The two men drifted toward the crowded table and worked their way through the bystanders. Hobe pointed out the men sitting with their old friend: Carl Mann, one of the owners; Charley

Rich, professional gambler; Captain Bill Massie, riverboat captain.

"They've become regular pals of his," added Hobe. Able noted the absence of Texas Jack, a man he had always liked.

For Able Guthrie to see his old friend sitting there again, in all his natural splendor, brought both a sense of pleasure and pain. The old gunfighter wasn't the same man he remembered back in Abilene five years earlier. The long, dark curly hair and coal-black mustache were the same. But the face, once angular and sharp, had filled out— almost puffy. And his dress was more that of a rich banker than a frontiersman: white shirt and necktie covered by a brocade vest and a long-tailed frock coat. Still, there were the ivory-handled Colts—butt forward—sticking out of a red sash waistband. But somehow they seemed more for show now.

And Able could tell by the way Bill was holding his cards and squinting that the eyes were bad. He felt the urge to turn and leave.

There was a break in the action as Captain Massie excused himself. Bill had already lost most of his chips and it was fairly plain to see his mood was growing gloomy. The others followed Captain Massie's lead. The crowd around the table began to break up too, leaving Curly Bill to sit alone under the shadowy glow of the oil lamp hung above the table. The light caused his skin to look yellow and waxy; the long, supple fingers drummed lightly on the table's top; the rosewater combed through his hair glistened as though he had been standing out in the rain.

"Howdy, Bill," said Hobe. The legend's head snapped up from the small stack of chips he had been staring at. He was squinting noticeably. "It's Hobe Waters, Bill, and another old pard of yours, Able Guthrie." Both men stepped into the light to make it easier.

Curly Bill stood to his full height, just a shade over six feet, slightly taller than Hobe and equal to Able.

"Well, kiss my sweet sister's dear ass!" he exclaimed. "I thought you two boys would be keeping company with the devil himself by now." They shook hands all around and Bill invited them to sit.

They talked of old times, and card games, and adventures that each had had since last they met. They expressed wonderment at how fate had led them all to Deadwood to be together again—to relive old times again! And when the others returned after a while to resume the card game, Bill waved them off in that inimitable way of his.

Curly Bill then ordered more whiskey for the three of them and the hours drifted away like autumn leaves being carried by the wind.

Somewhere in the wee hours, when even the

hardiest of hell-raisers had long since gone off to seek a bunk or soft place to lay their heads, Bill became maudlin. His two companions, their heads thick with liquor, listened with compassion as Bill spoke of his new wife back in New York.

"She can walk a tightrope frontwards and back," he said, his expressive eyes misting over. "Got balance like a cat. Ain't never seen a woman could ride a horse like her, neither." He was like a little boy telling it.

"She is a fine catch for an old hound like me," he told them. "Oh, you wouldn't exactly run over yourself at the sight of her, that's true. By most standards she is not a beauty. She don't fall into the same class, looks wise, as Billye Harrison over in Abilene, or even Chicago Jo— you remember Josephine Hensley, over in Helena don't you?" He searched their slack faces for assurance before continuing his litany.

"No, my Cynthiana couldn't rival any of them ladies in pure looks. But then they are all whores of the first rate. Hell!" he exhorted. "They were good old girls, weren't they?" Able and Hobe agreed that they were indeed.

Hobe said, "I heard Lillie killed herself by drinking poison, and Billye married a lawyer and lives in a twenty-room house." Bill said hurrah for her and he wished all the other girls could do as well as Billye had. They raised a toast in remembering.

"Boys," said Bill, "soon as I get a sizable poke together, I'm bringing the missus out—going to settle here permanent. I've got a feeling Deadwood is my last stop—there's something urgent about this place." Bill's face went all dreamy, like he was watching angels gather. Hobe and Able both felt pleased for him. He was a good man, tried and true. Able was thinking how Bill was getting too old to carry the past around with him much longer. Fact was, they all were. Maybe Deadwood was the best place for him, maybe he'd get a lasting peace here. A fellow deserved at least that much out of life.

It seemed less than possible, but the first light of morning was mousing through the windows and along the floorboards before they realized it. The bartender had crawled up on top of the mahogany bar and was sleeping like a baby.

Able pulled the railroader's watch from his pocket and read the hands. "Damn, boys, it's nearly six in the morning." He wound the stem.

Hobe groaned: "Dear lord, I've got to make rounds yet."

Bill just sat there with a beatific smile on his face, handsome as a racehorse. Able was pretty sure he had not been this drunk or tired in about twenty years—but then he forgot about Abilene and all those other times when he and Hobe and Curly Bill had tore it down.

"Bill, it has been a pleasure," he finally said,

pushing his chair away from the table. "I hope to hell that we will not be so long in crossing trails again." Curly Bill extended his hand, and in shaking it, Able noted that the flesh was smooth but the grip firm as ever.

"A man ain't much without good pards in this world," said Curly Bill. "You two fellows are counted among the best, in my book."

The door rattled open just as Hobe was shaking hands with Bill. A short, stout man wearing fancy beaded buckskins, moccasins, and a broad-brimmed beaver hat pinned up on one side, stepped inside the saloon. It was Texas Jack, Bill's most recent and constant companion. Both Able and Hobe knew Texas Jack as a good and decent man and greeted his arrival cordially.

"Looks as though you may have to assist our darling Bill back to his tent," said Hobe.

"I'm afraid so," sighed Texas Jack reaching out with both arms to help the stupefied Curly Bill gain his feet.

"Bill, you sure can be a caution," chided Texas Jack.

"I know it, Jack," murmured Bill, "But ain't living legends supposed to be sort of wild, and innocent of their sins?" said Bill in mock derision of his own status. Texas Jack simply smiled as he draped one of Bill's long arms around his neck and helped guide him toward the door. Suddenly, Bill stopped and lurched halfway around, nearly knocking Texas Jack over. The famous gunman eyed his two old comrades through eyes that narrowed in focusing. "We'll meet again," he said melodramatically, sweeping his free arm out to the side. "And you boys remember one thing— always sit with your tailside to the wall." He waved them adieu and they watched him and Texas Jack disappear through the door and out into the morning. The silence and the emptiness of the room with Bill's absence made it feel like ghosts had come to call.

They parted company outside, Hobe trying his damnedest to look dignified and walk a straight line while starting out his rounds.

Able turned in the opposite direction back to the boardinghouse. He took notice of how, at this hour, the town lay silent. A mist had enveloped the surrounding hills. The air was fresh and still. *Mornings were the way the world should always be,* he told himself. *Peaceful.* If there was one good thing in life, it was mornings.

# CHAPTER 5

He dreamed of the war. It was a dream that choked off his air and made him sweat his sheets wet, and it always felt like falling off a cliff.

The dream had his command surrounded in a woods that was being torn apart by cannon. Everything the Confederates could pour into the woods they did: grapeshot, shell, chain. Metal that ripped the flesh of men and horses and twisted their dying screams around the broken stumps of trees. BOOM! BOOM! BOOM! The cannon's pound became the pounding on his door and shook him from dreams of death to the coolness of his room.

"Able, it's me, Hobe," came the voice on the other side of the door. "I got a peck of trouble. I need to talk to you!"

Able fought off the stupor of sleep mired in heavy drink and struggled to right himself in the bed.

The fist banged down hard on the door again. "Able, you awake in there? Hurry, man, I ain't got all day!"

The lean man found his footing and turned the

key in the lock. Hobe quickly stepped inside and pushed the door closed behind him.

"What time is it, anyway?" asked Able, trying to shake the cotton from his head.

"A little after nine," replied Hobe, his nervousness apparent.

Able sat heavily on the bed and rested his head in the palms of his hands. "What's got you so jittery?" he asked the pacing Hobe. The lawman had walked to the small window and looked down on the street briefly and then had begun to pace the smallness of the room.

"Able, I wouldn't have come here if this hadn't involved you—and I sure wish to hell that it didn't. I didn't come to ask for your help, neither. . . ."

"Hobe, why don't you just spit out what it is you're getting at and let me decide how much of this I may want."

"Fair enough. The Deadwood Bank & Trust has been taken down. I don't know for how much yet, but it's a sour deal all the way around."

"How's that involve me?" asked Able, a nagging feeling crawling up his spine.

"Able, I already rode out to Ben Matters's place to inform him that his bank was robbed." Hobe paused and took a deep breath. "I found Ben inside his woodshed, his brains blowed out."

Hobe had said it directly and was watching carefully the look on his friend's face. The sharp looks lifted from the cupped hands slowly. Then the clear gray eyes lifted to meet his own. He saw the jaw muscles knot near the ridge of jaw-bone.

"And Annie?"

"Nowhere to be found, Able. I searched the whole place."

Able felt a tightness in his gut as though some-one had punched him there. "You saying she's missing?"

"It appears to be the case," replied Hobe. "One thing more," he continued, "their colored hand is missing too."

"You believe he had something to do with the robbery?"

"It'd be hard to believe otherwise."

"And he kidnapped Annie?"

Anxiety and stale booze caused him to sweat; he wiped his brow with a blue bandanna. "I can only guess that he did, seeing as how they're both gone."

Able was painting a picture in his mind as he dressed, a picture of his former wife: the tumble of auburn hair that fell past her shoulders when untied; the way her smile had a way of warming him better than any fire could; the way her skin smelled like lilac blossoms. And the picture also caused him to remember how, because she had wanted more than someone who dropped in every once in a blue moon—just long enough to get clean and rested and loved enough—how she had finally asked him for a divorce and he had given it to her. He gave her the divorce because he loved her too much not to. It was maybe the only thing she'd ever asked him for—and he couldn't say no to her. And he remembered giving himself hell about it for a long time afterward. After getting shot in the war and, later, divorced, it didn't seem as if anything would ever turn out just right for him.

By the time he heard she had married the banker in Deadwood, he had pretty much convinced himself that he was over her. But the news ate at him for a week.

He hadn't stayed steady with any woman in all that time because he never could find one that compared to Annie. And as he admitted to friends, he tried enough ladies to know there wasn't another like her. And in that time since they divorced, he had tried his hand at many things—farming, clerking, working in mines, and hauling freight—there wasn't any of it worth a lick as far as he was concerned. He finally decided to do what he was best at, using his courage and skill with a gun. He hired himself out for anything near legal and whatever suited his temperament or financial need at the time. After busting his back for other men, he decided too, that he'd only do what he wanted for the rest of his life.

It wasn't by accident that he showed up in

Deadwood nearly a year ago. It helped that his old friend Hobe was the law there and gave him an excuse to come riding in. And he had promised himself that he would stay away from her—maybe just see her once—maybe just for a few minutes.

As far as her new husband, the man wouldn't know Able from a mule skinner. And Able had promised himself to keep it that way.

But promises made and promises kept were two different things entirely.

He could no more stay away from her than stop breathing. And late one morning he had found it convenient to ride out by her place.

She was hanging wash on a line of rope, and she knew it was him from the way he rode—slightly off kilter because of his hip.

He walked his horse to a small picket fence that surrounded the yard and sat there looking down at her. She wanted to tell him to turn around and leave about as much as she wanted to be standing there looking like a dumpy hausfrau. Her sense of decency wouldn't allow her to invite him to step down, however. And her aching for him wouldn't invite him to leave without speaking. So they talked there, he on his horse, and she standing with the billow of laundry at her back. And somehow they both knew that it wasn't going to be a mere one-time visit.

"You are a man who makes me afraid of

myself," she told him one warm afternoon as they lay on a blanket in a meadow full of buttercups and soft grass.

Her softness and beauty seemed to have doubled each time they were together again. And there on the blanket and every time afterward, he craved her more than he had anything in his life.

"It's good that you have not changed your ways," she told him. "If you had, and you were about all the time, I'm afraid I could not stay married to Ben—I would want you too much. My only safety comes in knowing that even if you wanted to change, you couldn't. Some new adventure would come and drag you off sooner or later."

He tried to tell her he was ready for her now, ready for being together. He talked to her about his desire to save enough money to buy the place down in Arizona. But she shook her head at his efforts.

"Not until you are too old to ride a horse, or that hip of yours becomes too bad to let you ride. Maybe then you'll settle down but we'll both be too old by then," she told him. "My only sadness comes in knowing that you'll probably die somewhere far off and I will never know it. But then, maybe knowing it would only hurt more. You've brought me enough hurt, God knows."

She saw how her words affected him and quickly added, "But you have brought me plenty enough joy, too. Like now and for these last few weeks since you came calling."

He remembered how, at moments like that he felt overwhelmed by his love for her. They both knew that the way things were, their love was limited to clandestine meetings that always left them wanting more of the happiness and less of the sadness.

Able pulled on his other boot and stood.

"Tell me about this Negro hired man," he said, to Hobe breaking his reverie.

"Don't know a whole lot about him, other than Ben and Annie took him in one day about a month ago. Said he walked all the way from Kansas and was for some sort of land work. Ben told me he was impressed with the fellow's sincerity. Ben said the black told him he had fought in the war and fought Indians out in Texas and Colorado after that. Told Ben that it was hard for a colored to get decent work no matter what he had done in the past. Hell, Ben was soft about helping folks—Annie too, you know that."

"Is that it, he just came in to town one day and they hired him?"

"That's about all I know, he pretty much stayed to himself out there. Came in once or twice with Ben to get groceries and one time for lumber. Ben didn't talk much about him other than what I told you, and I didn't ask—wasn't no reason to, really. The only other thing I can tell you is, he's as big as a steam engine and dark-skinned."

"So you figure it was this . . . what'd you say his name was?"

"Luther. Luther Pride."

"So you figure it's this Pride that is responsible?"

"Don't know how else to figure it, Able. Ben's killed, the bank robbed, and Pride and Annie are both missing. I don't think I need to call a committee to figure it out."

Hobe tried hard to keep his concern from showing too strongly across his face. He was a stocky man who had the color of someone who'd worked his whole life in coal mines. His black hair, chopped short, appeared never to have had a comb run through it. And his eyes were like spuds of coal themselves. And when he got concerned over something, his naturally dark countenance grew even more stormy looking.

"Thing is," continued Hobe, "the lead dogs of this town have already put me on notice; this ain't no posse job. I'm considered the law here—the only law they'll pay for—and I'm responsible to get the money back."

Able took note that there was no mention of justice and finding Annie.

"And what are these fellows feeling about bringing back a murderer and kidnapper?"

Hobe rubbed the thick part of his jaw. "I have

to be honest with you, Able, these are men who wear paper collars and take a piss sitting down. They ain't concerned about more'n the money right now. The rest of it they just figure is bad luck."

"Bad luck!"

"I know what you're feeling, Able. I feel no less the same. Truth is, though, they pay my wages. A man my age and background don't find steady work every day of the week, or some that don't call for sitting in a saddle all day long and sleeping nights on the ground. . . ."

Able held up a palm. "You don't have to explain your circumstances to me, Hobe. We've rode too many trails together. Situations switched, I'd most likely feel the same."

"I just want you to know," replied Hobe, "I aim to do everything I can to bring back Annie and the money, even if Pride can't be found."

"I'm going with you—you know that."

"I hadn't figured otherwise, but I'll try just as hard to get her back whether you go or not."

"Hobe, like I said, you don't have to explain yourself to me."

The two men stared at each other for a long moment.

"Able, I want to clear the air about something before we leave here."

The lean man adjusted his gun belt on his narrow hips. "Say it."

"I know it ain't my business, but seeing as how I feel obligated to uphold whatever damn law there remains in this-here part of the country, I want your word that you won't let revenge kill a prisoner if I get the chance to bring in Pride."

"Since when did you get so damn awful full of righteousness, Hobe?"

"I just figure that if this badge don't stand for something, why wear it?"

"I give you my word, as much as I know I can. It depends on what harm he may have done her." Hobe drew a deep breath. Just getting that much from Able Guthrie, considering the circumstances, seemed a measure of their friendship and respect for what each felt he had to face.

"Your word's good enough. Let's go find the lady."

# CHAPTER 6

There were five of them sitting around the fire, blankets pulled up around their shoulders. First light was pushing back the shadows of the waning night. It was a meager fire at best. The air and ground were damp from night's dew, and overhead, thick, swollen clouds roiled the air with a promise of rain. Smoke from the fire was languid and barely rose above their heads.

Hap Patterson squatted on his haunches and eyed the others of his group. Sitting directly across from him with his eyes closed was Jim Buck. Next to Jim sat Lamar Eddings, a half-witted brute.

Hap looked at Luther Pride, whose silence made Hap uncomfortable. Pride sat next to Annie Matters, Hap's sister. Her auburn hair was twisted back in a tangled knot, her pretty face dirty from two days' riding and a lack of wash water. She looked worn, but like the black man, had barely spoken a word since the ordeal had begun.

Hap had wanted to talk to her, to justify it better, what he did and why. But each time he had sought out her attention, she had eyed him with a cold hatred that left no doubt in his mind that she wasn't ready to try to see his side of things. Still, he wanted her to know he hadn't enjoyed using her trust to take down the bank. But it had been just too damn much of a golden goose to pass up.

They should reach the Badlands by tomorrow night. If by then they weren't being trailed, he'd have Jim Buck kill Pride before they headed south to Nebraska Territory. Once there, Hap figured to break up the gang, put his sister on a stage to wherever she wanted to go—Deadwood included—and make sure she had enough of the loot to see her through the times ahead. In the meantime, he'd find out just how much of what he had heard about San Francisco was true.

He couldn't help but gloat over the genius of the plan he'd pulled off, in spite of having to use his own kin to do it. He had been dreaming of it ever since he'd heard that Annie had married a banker. It just had taken him a while to work out the details. When he had explained it all to Jim Buck and Lamar Eddings, they announced him the brightest fellow they had ever come across. And they each volunteered to shoot it out to the end, if it came to gunplay.

Hap Patterson knew the two to be casual about killing; it was that affinity that caused him to recruit the pair. Hap himself had only killed one man; that had been enough for him not to want to do it again.

51

There had been a dispute over a card game with an unarmed farmer. When Hap pulled the trigger on him, the man screamed, "Oh, my God!" and soiled himself as blood leaked through the fingers pressed over his gut. He begged for somebody to go get his wife, as he lay dying. In the final seconds, he rolled his eyes over to look into the face of his killer. Hap's hand was shaking as he stared down at the dying man.

The affair had disgusted him enough so that he vowed to himself if there was ever a need to do any more killing, he'd have someone else do it, someone more suited for it.

He had found Jim Buck swamping out saloons in Lead; not the sort of job that would cause one to suspect the violent nature of the man. Hap had been cooling his heels in the Blue Duck saloon the day Jim stopped emptying spittoons long enough to kill two men in a fight. What was most impressive to Hap about the event was that Jim wasn't packing a weapon and didn't appear especially strong. One of the men, a blacksmith, got unlucky enough to get his neck snapped in a twist of arm and hands that was too quick to see. The other fellow, a speaking acquaintance of the smith's, was gutted with his own blade. The whole thing was quick, start to finish: a slur tossed carelessly; a scuffle; the grunting snap of bone; a flash of knife blade. And two men slumped dead on the floor like boys taking a noon nap.

A quick trial was convened and the verdict was innocent due to self-defense. But the judge warned Jim to clear out of Lead. When Hap offered the ex-swamper a chance to throw in with him for a percentage of whatever came their way Jim acted like a spinster who had just been proposed to. Hap inquired of his new gang member if he knew of anyone else with the backbone who would like a similar opportunity. Hap stated further that he himself would cover all expenses until they came into some money.

"I do know a fellow over in Mud Butte—my cousin's boy—he might fit the bill," said Jim. "He ain't got all his punkin seeds planted, if you know what I mean, but he's big as an ox and loyal as a hound. I seen the sum-a-bitch lift up a buckboard on his back over a fifty-cent bet."

"Has he got the grit for outlawing?" asked Hap.

"I don't know that he's ever croaked anybody, but I believe he might if you was to pay him hard money."

"Let's say we ride over and have a look at him and find out if he'd be interested in joining up with us," said Hap, liking how the thought of having his own gang seemed to settle in his mind.

"I'm for it," said Jim Buck. "Last time I seen that boy, he had no shoes to put on his feet and he was eating spuds he dug up out of the ground with his toes. The boy's an eater. He'd most likely have to dig all day long, a boy that size."

Lamar Eddings was everything his cousin had said, leastways in appearance. Whereas Jim Buck was thin and wiry as a fence, Lamar was tall and fat. The dullard stood his ground near a pile of fresh-dug turnips and watched cautiously as the two men rode up. Hap allowed Jim to break the ice.

Jim walked his horse up until its chest was near even with Lamar's shoulder. It took a spell for Lamar to recognize his kin, and when he did, he grinned like a fed possum.

Jim explained that Mr. Patterson here needed an extra hand he could trust to work for him. "I'm his main gun, of course," he further explained. "You'd be under me, and you'd have to take orders clear as rain water, without hesitation, from me or him. You understand?" Lamar nodded his head up and down.

"You do all that, and the pay would be good enough to buy you a pair of regular shoes, and enough grub so's you wouldn't have to suffer on a place like this anymore."

Lamar listened hard, glancing from his cousin to Hap Patterson and then to the tops of his toes.

"Of course, you know," added Jim, "working for us might mean you'd have to hurt people if it came to that—if Mr. Patterson or me asked you to—could you do that, Lamar?" Lamar raised his eyes while just barely moving his head. "Well, can you or can't you?" quizzed Jim Buck.

" 'Cause if you can't, maybe you ain't the fellow we need." Lamar's head came up like he had been beaned by something.

"I hurt a man once," he said, full of pout. "Hurt him till he weren't able to walk no more." It was a confession that seemed to lie on the air like a coffin in an empty room.

"How come you to do that to some fellow?" This time it was Hap Patterson who spoke.

Lamar looked unevenly at the man in the shiny shirt and black britches. He recollected he had never seen a man dressed that fancy before. White webs of spittle formed in the corners of Lamar's mouth as he spoke. " 'Cause he gigged a frog I had."

"Your pap own a horse?" asked Hap.

Lamar nodded that he did.

Hap pulled twenty dollars from his pocket and handed it down to Lamar. "Go give this to your daddy for his horse and tell him you got a job."

"What if he won't take this for his horse?" asked Lamar staring at the paper money in his hands.

"You remember what I told you!" said Jim. "About doing what you're told. Just do it, and if the sum-a-bitch don't want the money then bring it back, but come riding a horse either way. Now git!" The two riders watched as Lamar stuck a turnip in each pocket of his coveralls and trundled off toward the distant house.

Now they sat, five diverse souls around a fire that was more smoke than warmth. The air was heavy and damp and the smoke languished, burning their nostrils and irritating their eyes.

They pulled blankets up over them to keep out the smoke as best they could. Lamar fumbled under his blanket with food he had stored ever since Hap Patterson had recruited him off his pap's farm. Now he sat, contented with two strips of beef jerky and three hardtack biscuits and a raw turnip.

Jim Buck had grown weary of the chase and wasn't feeling keen about sitting under a blanket on a damp evening in the middle of nowhere. Jim Buck had wanted to kill the Negro at the same time as he had killed Ben Matters, but Hap was dead set against it. Hap had said that they needed to keep him alive in order to make it look like he had been the one to rob the bank and kill the banker. "It only makes sense to pin it on the colored boy, don't it?" he had said. "This way it'll look like he done the whole thing and kidnapped Annie in the doing. Hell, they'll be looking for him, not for us."

Hap had gone on to tell Jim Buck that once they hit the Badlands, Jim Buck could kill Pride. "They ain't nobody'll find that fellow down in the Badlands—and if they do, we'll be clear out of the territory."

Hap did not include the half-wit in the revelation of his plans. "No use explaining all this to Lamar," he'd confided to Jim Buck. "That boy wouldn't remember it anyway. Once we get to Nebraska Territory, things will be roses."

Annie Matters hunkered under her blanket and burned with anger toward her brother who sat across from her. She had grown to hate the sight of him in these last two days. She had always known him to be of slim hope, as someone who couldn't or wouldn't do honest labor. And though he was only her half-brother, she had practically raised him. Now she realized more than ever how different he and she were. He was a Patterson. She and her ma and pa were Jordons. And when her pa died, her ma had married old man Jubal Patterson who, at nearly seventy years old, had still been able to get her ma pregnant.

The baby lived but her ma didn't. At the age of nine, and with no other family, she'd stayed on and raised Hap. And by the time she had left on the back of Able Guthrie's horse, she had already seen firsthand the wastrel ways of Hap Patterson. Lazy and no account, in spite of his charm. But in spite of herself, she could not totally ignore news of him, or fail to send him a present at Christmas or on his birthday. Now she wished she hadn't.

Her mind kept rushing back to two weeks ago when Hap and the two men with him came riding up in her front yard. She had been both happy to see him and uncomfortable with his showing up unannounced and with a couple of no-accounts.

But she had consented to allow them to camp out in the barn for a few days. He'd told her he did not come to intrude . . . just wanted to see his darling sister one more time. They were all headed off to mine silver down in New Mexico, didn't know when he might get by this way again. "Hell, sis, this Deadwood is a long shot from anywhere—must get colder than sin in the winter," he said and laughed.

And so she had let them stay. In fact, Ben insisted that they stay. He was such a good and kind man. How many times she wished she had the heart and soul of her husband. And now, in thinking about him, tears welled in her eyes. For it was not only the fact that these men had robbed him and taken advantage of his trust and kindness that disturbed her so. It was the fact that she too had broken his trust by not turning Able away the day he rode up to the yard. Ben's having been so wronged by her brother and by her made her want to scream.

She stared at Hap through a break in the blanket and he saw her looking. A part of him wanted to go to her, but it had been such a long time ago that they were family and he didn't feel that he owed her much more than to take care of her until they reached Nebraska. He wouldn't allow any harm to come to her—he did owe her that much for certain.

She watched him until he turned his gaze from her. Annie remembered the night of the robbery. Earlier she had cooked a supper for all of them because Hap had announced that the next morning he and his friends would be leaving for New Mexico. Up until that time, they had all been perfect gentlemen, even helping with chores.

It was funny what she remembered about that night, things like the dinner of venison, boiled potatoes, and a rhubarb pie so sweet and tart it made you smile. And it did seem like family with Ben sitting at one end of the table and Hap at the other and she between them.

After supper, the men had gone out on the porch to smoke and she could hear them speaking the way men do when they're relaxing, and she could smell the cigar smoke drifting in through the kitchen window while she worked on the supper dishes. Hap had walked back in and told her how much he had appreciated all Ben's and her hospitality. And then he had stared at her for a long moment and finally sighed and told her that he was taking Ben into the bank and was going to fill up with money as many grain sacks as he could carry.

She laughed and said that he shouldn't be joking about such things because Ben might not understand. "He takes his position very seriously," she had told Hap. And then the small man came in with a pistol pressed to Ben's temple.

"I ain't fooling, Annie," Hap had said. "It ain't like I'm robbing you or Ben—it's the bank we're taking down. I want you to be cool as cucumbers about it."

It was all matter-of-fact coming out of his mouth. And poor Ben, he had stood wide-eyed and pale as linen. And then the other one, Lamar, came in with Luther. There was a gun pointed at his head too.

"Ben, you follow along with this thing, and everyone will make out all right," said Hap. "You don't, I can't guarantee what these boys might take it in their heads to do here. You cooperate, I'll move these boys out without a hitch. You following what I'm saying?"

She had found herself screaming at Hap to stop it! And he let her carry on for about half a minute and then he cocked back his pistol and placed it against Ben's chin and she shut up.

A shove of wind pushed a cloud of smoke into her and caused her to lurch into a coughing spell. She saw Luther start to get up to come to her when the small man tossed off his blanket and pointed his gun. "Sit down there, darkie. The lady will be all right without any of your help!" The black man eased back down.

Luther Pride had seen lots of white trash in his

time. Trash was trash, no matter what color it came in. It seemed like no matter where he went, he was always running into trouble with white people. When he had hired on with Ben Matters, he did so because the banker and his wife had treated him "regular." It was uncommon. Ben had proved to be as decent a man as Luther had ever encountered. Annie was always pleasant and had a kind word for him. It did not seem right that she would have kin the likes of Hap Patterson.

Luther sat back down, his passive eyes belying the anger that was in him. He knew that sooner or later, these men would kill him—if not her too. Even since the ordeal had begun, he had waited for a chance to do something in his and Annie's favor. But these were cautious men and they kept a short rope on him day and night. Especially the one they called Jim Buck. He knew that little gunman would gladly pull the trigger on him if for nothing more than his color.

But Luther knew that no matter how vigilant they were, there would be at least one brief moment of letdown. He'd be patient until that moment.

Annie Matters saw the look of impassiveness on Luther's face, as though he were obeying some command from within. As she watched him, she realized that she knew very little about the man. He had always affected a quiet, respectful manner with her and her husband, but she had always sensed, too, that he was not a shallow man with a weak soul. Some men possessed a strength that did not need to be spoken of or proved, but like a deep, calm river's surface, had a power flowing beneath it that could be dangerous.

And like water rushing against river rocks, although its path is momentarily diverted it sooner or later wears away its obstacle. Right at this moment, Luther Pride was her only source of comfort—her only hope.

# CHAPTER 7

Annie clung to the hope that her husband was all right. The night of the robbery Hap and Ben had ridden back into the yard with two heavy gunny sacks tied to the pommel of Hap's saddle. Ben looked haggard and afraid, slumped in his saddle.

Their arrival brought the others outside, she and Luther escorted at gunpoint.

Hap marveled at how easy it had all been. "Easy as cracking walnuts with a hammer," he told the others. "Hell, I think maybe there ain't never been a bank robbery as quiet as this one." She had tried to go to her husband, to help him down off his horse, but Jim's hand around her arm was like iron claws.

"What's the take?" Jim wanted to know.

"Hard to say, you think I sat down and counted it? But it's enough that you won't ever have to swamp out another saloon again. And Lamar there won't ever have to dig another turnip up with his toes either," said Hap. "Boys, I can't see nothing but moonlight and roses ahead of us now, thanks to old Ben here and that fat bank of his."

"It's not so fat anymore," said Lamar, patting the sacks like they were tonight's supper.

"See there, Jim, ol' Lamar's becoming a right proper badman."

"A meaner sum-a-bitch I ain't never seen before," Jim said jovially, his hot, foul breath nearly smothering Annie.

"Should I kill the nigger now, Mr. Hap?" asked Lamar.

Hap's buckskin danced halfway around and Hap snapped back on the reins to settle him. "Lamar, you got a soft spot in your brain big as a snapping turtle, you know that?" Hap quickly shot a look at his sister, and then, as if to play it down as a joke, ordered the oaf to apologize to her for scaring her with such rough, stupid talk.

"Go on, Lamar, tell Annie you was acting the fool and that you ain't going to kill nobody!"

Lamar looked almost tearful over the rebuke.

His brutish face turned toward hers but he kept his eyes lowered the whole time. "I ain't gonna kill nobody, miss. I was . . . I was just funning with you is all."

She wanted to scream.

But she didn't. Instead she found herself begging for all of them. Begging Hap and the others to go and leave them alone. Take the money, take anything in the house, just please, please go. Hap told her he'd do that if everyone cooperated for the next few days and went along with his plan.

"You got to be patient here," he told them. "You got to be calm as clams or there can't be no guarantees."

Ben had, after a time, found his voice, and tried to reason with the men. "You leave us be, and I'll promise, because of these two innocent souls, that I will not go for the law, or be a party to search for you or your men."

"Well now, that's a start in the spirit of cooperation, I'd say," replied Hap. "Thank you, Ben. And I wish it were as easy as all that, but at least me and you see things along the same track."

"You mean you won't just ride off and let it go where it stands now?"

"Like to, that's a fact. But until we clear the territory, I'll need some insurance that you'll remain a man of your word. I'll take Annie and the black along just to see that you remain loyal to the idea." Ben Matters started to protest and Jim cocked back the hammer of his Remington. It sounded like a bone breaking.

She remembered telling her distraught husband that it was all right, that regardless of the situation, Hap was still her kin and he wouldn't let anything happen to her.

Hap ordered them to get ready to ride. He allowed Annie to throw a few clothes in a valise, and told Lamar to go round up as much grub as wouldn't spoil on a ride. He had Jim take Luther

Pride over and saddle up the necessary horses, including the iron-gray Tennessee walker that was Annie's pride and joy. And when all was ready, he ordered Jim to stay behind for a while with Ben Matters, just in case anyone had "wised up about the bank," as he had put it.

Ben looked at her helplessly as she kissed him good-bye. Hap and Jim had walked a distance—just out of hearing range—to speak to each other.

The four rode off. After an hour or so Jim Buck caught up with them. Hap assured Annie that Ben was all right, but how much weight could she place on the word of a liar?

# CHAPTER 8

Hobe Waters wiped sweat from his forehead with a kerchief while he waited for Able to finish his inspection of the body of Ben Matters.

The single shot in the back of the head had exploded out through the dead man's cheekbone. The smell of death was already beginning to foul the air inside the woodshed.

They stepped back outside and closed the door. "Before we head out," said Hobe, "I'll stop back in town and send some men out to take poor Ben on into the funeral parlor."

The two then inspected the rest of the grounds. There were three pretty worn horses in the corral, and a big yellow tomcat the size of a bear cub that trailed them around. Other than that, there were no other signs of any living thing.

They crossed the yard several times, searched the inside of the house, saw that some of the cupboards had been ransacked, but otherwise, everything else seemed undisturbed.

"What's your assumption?" asked Able.

"Looks as though the black robbed the bank, killed poor old Ben, and kidnapped Annie. Maybe he took her out there and left her somewhere." He pointed off toward the forested distance. "There sure ain't nobody else here."

"You got any ideas on where a black man could carry off a white woman and not be noticed or questioned?"

"Not any place safe as I can think of," replied Hobe. "But it'd seem to me the most logical place to head from here would be up to the Canadian border." Hobe was fingering a crease in the high-crown hat he wore.

"That would seem to be the bet."

"Does it seem odd to you that a fellow would do the one thing that *would* draw the most attention to him? I can see him wanting her. Hell, any man might, but why take her along? It would be like breaking wind in church, everyone would take notice."

"A man that's desperate does desperate things," said Able. "A man like that don't take time to look at tomorrows." His jaw muscles worked into knots as he spoke. His eyes searched the distance as though he hoped to see something that instinct told him wasn't there.

"There must be a hundred different ways to get to the border from here, and with a whole day's lead, I'd say we'd be just as lucky falling down a well and not hurting ourselves as to pick the exact way they went."

Able knew Hobe was right.

"If we start out heading in the wrong direction," Hobe continued, "that'll just put us more wrong than if we sit here and do nothing." Both men brooded in silence.

"Preacher Bill!" Able said of a sudden.

"Hell, yes! Why didn't I think of that?" said Hobe, slapping his Stetson back on his head. And then just as suddenly, the excitement went out of the lawman and he fell glum. "I forgot, Able, Preacher ain't a tracker anymore—his choosing."

"Why so?"

"It's something that happened before you came back to Deadwood, and before I became the law."

"Seeing as how things are, maybe you could explain what it is that would keep us from at least asking him for his help," said Able.

"Well, you know when he was younger he raised more hell than all the women east of the Mississippi raised kids. And it was down in New Orleans that he got into a fight with a Cajun pimp who shot Billy in the head with a derringer. But somehow the bullet from that pimp's pistol didn't do more than bounce off his forehead and knock him out. He said when he came to he knew right away it was some sort of message from the Almighty to go straight." Hobe paused long enough to draw breath. He could see Able's impatience.

"I'm leading up to why I don't think Preacher

will help us, but you've got to know some of where he's come from to understand.

"Just before you came to Deadwood, and I became sheriff, Bill was hired on to track down a boy wanted for killing a girl child—she had been raped and thrown down a mine shaft. Everyone pretty much figured it was a kid named Ike Farrow. Ike had trouble figuring things out—he was a little shy of all his brains. But he was a good boy, seemed harmless enough, until they found that little girl. Somehow, nobody seems to remember exactly how, the blame got placed on Ike. He got wind of it and ran off, which only confirmed suspicion on him.

"Anyway, they hired Preacher Billy to track him down, which didn't take more than a day. They found Ike in a hole he had dug up in the hills." Hobe paused in his narration and shook his head.

"As it turned out, the posse turned into vigilantes and hung the boy from the first tree—all except Preacher Billy was for it. The really bad thing about the whole affair was that later, a miner name of Gratton confessed to killing the girl. Said he was drunk at the time. Afterward, his drinking gave him nightmares about it until he couldn't stand to live with himself no longer. They hung him too."

Hobe looked hard at his friend for a long second. "Preacher Billy never got over the fact he

70

tracked down an innocent man that the town wound up hanging. He said he'd never track down another man as long as he lived. You see, Able, even if this is a clear case of kidnapping and murder, Preacher Bill wouldn't saddle a horse to go after Luther Pride."

"Where's he live?"

"Back the other side of town. Not much more than a cabin in a clearing of tree stumps he uses for chairs on Sunday, and one big one he stands on to deliver fire-and-brimstone sermons to them that'll come listen," Hobe said. "He's married to a gal half his age, and they got twin baby boys no bigger than sugar bags."

"I got to ask him anyway," said Able. "He can tell me no if he wants, but I'm asking."

"We'll both ask," replied Hobe, mounting his coyote dun mare.

Bill West, or Preacher Billy as he was most often called, was sitting on the porch of his cabin, a heavy leather-bound Bible laid open across his lap. His eyes trailed along behind the movement of his forefinger as he read his way through a passage. He heard the approach of the two riders, but stayed with his reading from Isaiah.

". . . So He became their Savior. In all their affliction He was afflicted. And the Angel of His Presence saved them; In His love and in His pity He redeemed them."

They sat their mounts waiting for some form of recognition and an invitation to step down. It took awhile.

Finally Preacher Billy raised his head from the book, closed his eyes, and allowed his lips to move wordlessly. When he opened his eyes he acknowledged the two men sitting on a good-sized dun and a big chestnut gelding in his front yard. It was an old habit of his to notice the horses men rode and how they rode them. It was an old habit he was trying hard to break. That, and a few others only he and the Lord knew about.

Preacher squinted through the wire-rimmed spectacles perched on his hawk-nose. "Hobe, I see you brought along a familiar face—that you, Able Guthrie?"

Able leaned forward in the saddle, as though to give Preacher Bill the benefit. "It's me, Preacher Billy. Might I inquire as to your health these days?"

"Wonderful, Able. Simply wonderful. The Lord has provided me with strong limbs, an ample voice, and a fiery will. All the tools a man needs to spread the Good News. And if all that wasn't enough, the Almighty gave me a woman strong enough to help with chores, and bountiful enough to bear children." Preacher rose to his feet and placed both hands on the porch rail in front of him and leaned forward, as though he were standing in a pulpit.

"I congratulate you on your blessings," said Able, truly glad that there was at least one person on this earth who seemed happy and content with his lot in life.

A young woman appeared in the doorway of the cabin. Able judged her to be not more than seventeen or eighteen years of age. At each side she held the hand of a small child, towheaded boys who had the woman's looks. She did not come all the way out onto the porch, choosing instead to remain standing in the doorway. From what Able could see of her features, she was a winsome-looking woman with straight, light hair and angular features. She was also very pregnant.

She fixed her eyes first on Hobe Waters, and then on Able. Everything about her appeared shy, except for her intense, willful stare. One of the boys strained to leave her grasp, but she silenced him with a look. Able figured that Preacher Billy had done well in finding himself a wife.

"I invite you boys to step down and join me here in the shade of the porch," Preacher Billy said.

As they joined him on the porch, he offered them some cold bark tea. Hobe declined, but Able said bark tea sounded like just the thing. Mrs. Billy West and the two babies disappeared back into the cabin. Able assumed it was to get the tea, although Preacher Billy hadn't said a word about her getting it.

The two visitors sat quietly for a time trying to figure out just how to ask Bill about doing something they knew he probably wouldn't do. They didn't need to wait long. Preacher Billy was not a man to beat around the bush on a matter.

"I take it you two rascals have not suddenly decided to become righteous and bring yourselves all the way out here just so's I could take you down to the creek and baptize you personal?"

"No sir, we haven't," replied Hobe. "We come for something a whole lot different than that."

"Well, Hobe, you being the law, and Able, last I heard, you were still doing detective work, I'd guess you are here on either some official business, or something unofficial, but either way it involves needing a tracker."

"That's exactly why we're here, Preacher," said Able unable to be patient any longer now that the cat was out of the bag. But before he could speak the rest of it, Preacher held up his hand.

"We're old friends," began Billy, "but the fact of the matter is, I don't do any more tracking."

"Preacher Bill, I respect your resolve on the issue," said Able. "And I hope it wasn't breaking trust that Hobe told me about the last time you tracked a man and how all that turned out. But as a friend, I hope you'll hear me out before saying no. Listening can't be a sin, or a breaking of a vow."

"I reckon not, old friend," smiled Preacher

Billy, removing the wire-rimmed specs one ear piece at a time. "I'll listen, but I'm not your man."

Able told Bill how it was, what had happened, how they found Ben Matters shot through the head and how Annie and Luther were both missing and how they were pretty certain of what had happened. He didn't mention why it was eating him up inside about her; he figured Preacher didn't need to know that.

"We intend to run this fellow to ground, and when we do, there is every likelihood we may kill him—he'll be desperate when we catch him." Able paused in order to choose his next words carefully.

"Fact is, Preacher, whether you help us track him or not, sooner or later, we'll catch him. Your helping will get it done sooner, and I figure the sooner we can catch him, the better the odds are for Annie. The other truth is, you maybe could wind up saving both their lives by helping."

"How do you figure that?" asked Preacher.

"Because when we catch him, and if he has killed Annie, you might be the only one to talk me out of killing him."

Preacher hooked his glasses back on his ears and looked intently at the two men sitting on his porch. "You have anything to add to this, Hobe?"

"No sir, other than Able's telling you the truth. It's a bad situation that will only get worse the longer it goes on. I represent the law, but if Luther

Pride has killed her, there won't be either one of us in a mood to bring him back just to watch him hang. Your coming along could well be Annie's salvation, the colored's too."

Preacher stood, hooked his thumbs inside his vest pockets, and walked out into the yard. The two men on the porch watched him with growing impatience. He was nearly fifty years old and growing bald like a monk. And with the eyeglasses, white collarless shirt, and black pants, he looked like a preacher instead of the best damn tracker either one of them had ever known.

Preacher's wife reappeared carrying two glasses of tea. One she placed on a small table next to Preacher's Bible, the other she handed to Able. Their eyes met for a brief moment, and he could see nothing in the pale grayness of hers that welcomed him. He understood the look, he had seen it in other women in other times. Women who were about to share their men with other men, or with wars, or with other women. He had seen the same look in Annie's eyes every time he rode off. He had seen it the last time he had ridden off and the last time he'd returned. He had seen it just before she told him she was leaving him. He felt the ache he knew Preacher's wife to be feeling now.

Able sipped on the tea and traded glances with Hobe as they waited for Preacher to say something.

Slowly he turned and walked back to the porch, sunlight glinting off the wire rim of his specs. "I know Luther Pride," he said. "I find it hard to believe that such a man would do the things you have said. Even though we never broke bread together, nor knelt in prayer, he seemed a man of strong moral character—not the sort of man to murder and kidnap his benefactors. However, in my lifetime, I have learned to accept the fact that the love of money can cause a man to become something he normally ain't—it's been the case all through time. Maybe that's what happened to Luther Pride." He picked up the glass of tea in one hand and his Bible in the other.

"I'll need some time to chew on all this." He could read their faces. "I know you boys are in a hurry to start on this, but what you're asking of me is pulling me in two different directions at once. I need to discuss it with the Man up above, and with Inge—we got two babies and one nearly here. Give me an hour, I'll either meet you at Ben Matters's place or I won't. Either way, you'll know my answer." He turned and went inside.

# CHAPTER 9

Able paced the yard while Hobe paced the front porch of Ben's and Annie's house. Every few minutes Hobe took out his pocket watch, snapped open the gold lid and checked the time. He was a short, square man whose close-cropped black hair and thick eyebrows made him look dangerous. He had a choppy gait and even when he paced, his boots clomped across the boards as if he were marching. He was not given to frills and so his dress was simple: plain cotton shirt, cowhide leather vest, denim jeans, high-crowned brown Stetson. He also wore a Colt .45 with a six-inch barrel strapped to his hip. The one piece of dress he took thorough pride in was the nickle-plated badge that said Marshal, which he wore pinned to his vest. It was usually the first thing people noticed about him when they met. He liked the instant respect it drew from most of the people he encountered and dealt with. As for the rest, the drunks, the fighters, and rounders, the badge gave him the authority to deal with them in his own way—he liked that too.

He had been married once, but his wife had

caught the fever and died before they ever got the chance to know each other very well. He never met anyone else that had interested him in that way. He liked horses, and he liked some men, and he liked being the law. Beyond that, he didn't think about much more than whatever was facing him at the moment.

They heard loud braying and their pacing came to a stop. It was Preacher Billy riding a big, coffee-colored mule, its long ears twitching, its eyes big as powdered biscuits.

He rode up and pulled back on the reins and the mule stopped dead, took one or two steps backwards and stopped again. "You'll have to excuse Tom, here," said Preacher. "He's irritated over something I ain't figured out yet—he's been like this all the way over here." Preacher patted the animal's neck and spoke in soothing tones. The long ears seemed to be snapping up the words in back and switching them around to the front.

Hobe swung down off the porch and fell in step with Able as they walked over to greet Bill.

"Preacher, this means a lot to me personally, and I know that Hobe is equally obliged at your coming," said Able. Hobe nodded his agreement.

"Well, to be honest with you boys, I did some mighty hard praying and searched over my soul like it was a legal document. But not even that was enough. I still couldn't come up with an answer to all this."

"What was it that made you decide?" interrupted Hobe.

"It was my woman Inge that convinced me I should come."

"What did she say?" asked Able.

"She said an old man like me, with a wife and almost three babies, had no right whatsoever to go off chasing fugitives like I was some sort of wild buckaroo! She didn't say anything about me getting shot or stabbed, or maybe getting my head busted in in some fight. She said she was worried, at my age, I might fall off my mule and break my neck!

"Can you imagine that! Me falling off a mule when I was practically born in a saddle! It was right then when she started that speech that I knew I had to go—at least this one last time."

They all grinned like schoolboys.

"Don't get me wrong," continued Preacher. "I love Inge, she's a fine Swede woman, young and strong and willing. She just ain't ever quite adjusted to this country yet. Being left alone in it gives her the willies. I made arrangements for the neighbors to check in on her and the babies every day or so. I'm trying hard to be a God-fearing man, but pride is one sin I just haven't been able to shed yet."

Able was beginning to feel bad he had asked

Preacher to help. He remembered the times he had ridden off and left Annie, and how he had done it once too often. He wondered if any woman ever got used to being left alone, regardless of where she was.

"I suppose I have sat here and jawed enough," said Preacher, "let me have a look around."

Preacher walked straight to the corral and took note of the three horses that lazed within. "Two nags and a broom-tail," he muttered to himself. "Poor horseflesh indeed." He then set his focus on the ground in front of the gate. He traced a line back to the yard, walking half bent over so he could see better. He paused briefly in front of the porch and then walked down the lane leading out to the road. Able and Hobe followed. Preacher stood in the middle of the road and looked down it both ways, knelt on one knee and fingered places where there showed many hoof prints. Finally he stood, brushed off his knee, and asked: "Either Ben or Annie own a Tennessee walking horse?"

"Yes sir," replied Hobe. "It was Annie's pride and joy. Ben bought the animal from a plantation outside of Memphis—a wedding gift."

Able felt a stab of jealousy go through him.

Preacher called them over to where he was standing and knelt again. "You see here on the ground, the way this one set of prints cuts out to the side? That's the way a walker throws out his forelegs when he trots—like riding on pillows,

81

quite an experience." The other two men looked closer and saw it plainly. "All these tracks were made together, as far as I can tell. Four riders rode out together, including that walker." Preacher waited for that to sink in.

"There is one more piece to this puzzle," continued Preacher. "This last set of tracks is another body altogether. The first four up to this point were on a trot. This last one was cutting at a full-out gallop. You can tell by how deep the marks cut into the ground and the way the dirt is torn up. See there, stretched out at a full run," he said, pointing out the distance between each set.

"What's your sense tell you, Preacher?" asked Able.

"Seems to be saying that there was more than Luther in on this thing. And it could be that someone else is after them from the way that last set of prints seems to be riding. Other than that I can't say."

"Well, if someone is chasing them, it's nobody official," commented Hobe. "I'd know about it."

"It could be one waited behind as lookout, stayed awhile, then rode out," replied Preacher.

"It's hard to say exactly what we're dealing with now," said Able. "I know one thing certain, Annie's chances were poor to begin with, they're worse now." Able stared down the road.

"What's the fastest way to the Canadian border, Preacher?"

"Fastest way would be up the Belle Fourche trail, directly north. But I can't understand why you'd want to go there," quizzed the old tracker.

Guthrie swung up in the saddle and wheeled his gelding around to where Preacher and Hobe were still standing. He eyed the minister evenly. "What are you telling me?"

"I'm saying north ain't where they're headed. Belle Fourche trail would be in that direction," he said, pointing up past the house and toward the tall timber beyond. "It looks like these tracks are heading southeast."

"Meaning what, exactly?"

"Exactly is hard to say, but my guess is the Badlands."

# CHAPTER 10

A small cadre of men rode their horses through the broken landscape of the Badlands, the clatter of hooves echoing off the walls of rock and hills. They were an assorted bunch—grim faced and poorly dressed. Some carried pistols strapped to their waists or tucked inside their belts, others had rifles or shotguns laid across their saddles and tucked down in scabbards.

Their leader, a half-breed named English, rode at the front of the group. He was a big, powerful man with a square face, stringy black hair, and eyes as pale blue as robins' eggs. He wore a battered sombrero that looked like it had collected about all the dust it could carry, a leather vest, dirty cotton trousers tied around the waist with a rope, and a pair of torn moccasins. He rode a big, muscled gray whose tail had been braided.

Behind English rode Dog. His name was Bishop, but they called him Dog because he had made the mistake once of telling the others how he used to get twenty-five cents apiece for shooting stray dogs while he was a deputy marshal in

Leavenworth, Kansas. Bishop was thin as wire, barely standing five-six, but he was as fearless as English, and he had stood his share of violence and come through it okay. But age had made him slow and no one needed an old man whose only talent was shooting—no one except those who rode the other side from the law.

Behind Dog, riding side by side, were the Anger brothers, Earl and Edward—two Ohio lads who had tossed down their hoes one day in disgust, stolen what money their ma had saved under a board in the bedroom floor, and lit out for better times. It didn't take either one long to learn how to earn their way by sticking guns in people's faces and taking whatever was available. After the first few times, they both agreed it was something they were good at and something they enjoyed. They loved little else, except maybe to be drunk and mean. And when they weren't drunk and mean, they were sober and mean.

They were similar in looks: broad, round faces, narrow eyes, stuck-out ears, close-cut hair, and flat noses. They were the poorest dressed of the bunch, as well. Except for the black derby atop Earl's head, their attire consisted of linsey-woolsey shirts out at the elbows, woolen pants out at the knees, and brogan shoes out at the toes.

Bringing up the rear of the column was the last of them, Orley Parson. Other than English, the rest of the men kept their distance from him, and he, them. As usual, Orley was having difficulty riding. His body ached as he fought the desire to reach round in his saddlebags and pull out the little blue bottle of laudanum. There was barely a swallow left and he wanted to wait until the last possible minute before he fed his system.

Orley was a gangly stick of a fellow who looked like he'd hardly eaten since he was born. He had cadaverous eyes and his skin was so thin and pale that his veins looked like little blue rivers running through milk.

It wasn't unusual to see him ride off into the woods or out into a field and come back carrying a fistful of weeds or bark he would boil in water to drink. Said he could find no pleasure in eating dead flesh—it bogged down a man's mind and stomach. Sometimes he'd rub sage on his skin and breathe in smoke from the camp fire and then go lie out in the open on his back with his arms stretched wide and commence to hum. To everyone except English, Orley Parson was a spook.

But in English's eyes, Orley was special. Ever since he first found Orley Parson lying out in a field one day completely naked and humming to the sun, English knew that this skeletal-looking man was something unique. And indeed, he proved to be.

Orley kept a set of bones in his saddlebag, along with the little blue bottle of laudanum.

Whether the bones were human, as Orley claimed them to be, or animal was hard to say. But Orley used them to consult the Higher Orders and then to pass that knowledge along to English.

"I'll consult you free for a taste of your whiskey," Orley had offered on that first encounter. English let him drink from the bottle he had been carrying.

"Sit down here on the ground and let me get the bones," he'd ordered. "And leave the bottle uncorked."

Orley tossed the bones out on the ground between him and English, studied them, picked them up and tossed them again and studied some more. Then he carefully reached over and moved them around, took another hard pull on the whiskey bottle, and moved them some more. He did that until the whiskey was all gone and the sun felt like a hot poker on the back of English's neck.

"You are in good shape, my friend, the Higher Orders dictate it. Your next endeavor, which will be very soon from now, will be a favorable one."

"You drink all my whiskey and you speak gibberish—what you say to me, crazy man?" English demanded.

"First of all, my friend, you should not disavow what you don't fully understand. In other words, you're about to do something pretty important to you and you'll pull it off without a hitch."

English was awestruck. He had been planning on robbing a mine-company office of its payroll the next day. And here this strange fellow was practically predicting it.

"How do you know what English plans?"

"Don't know—the Higher Orders do, though—I consulted them," he said, pointing at the motif of bones on the ground.

Right then English decided that Orley should ride along with him and the others until after the mine office was taken down. The job went off as planned, with even more money than they had counted on. English figured he had a good thing cooking in Orley, and Orley knew he had a good thing in English.

Orley had come West after having studied medicine, religion, and all other fields of the human condition he could before being tossed out of Harvard College for "riotous acts" that consisted mainly of getting skunk drunk and setting the campus dining hall on fire in protest of "serving dead animals" for meals.

His father had insisted that Orley catch the next train west and even provided him with the ticket and five hundred dollars living money. There was no request for him to write home and tell his people how he was doing. Eventually he landed in San Francisco. First he found the opium dens, and later a doctor who was willing to sell him all the laudanum he could afford—which was considerable. "Portable and powerful, take all the unpleasantness right out of you," the doctor had said. "Works for pain of both kinds—a wondrous potion." What the doctor didn't mention was the fashion in which the body craved the stuff when it wasn't being supplied, and that enough never seemed enough.

The one thing Orley's brief but learned stay at Harvard did teach him was to develop an innate understanding of people and what motivated them. In English's case, it was simple. He was a man of mixed blood—which meant he wasn't accepted by anybody. He was a man of little education but not necessarily low intelligence, someone who had a well-developed instinct for survival. He ruled by toughness and his willingness to kill or be killed. Fear was as alien to English as bravery was to most men. English would walk through a barn full of fire and bullets if there was something inside he wanted.

In Orley Parson's initial assessment, English had only one weakness—his ability to believe the unbelievable. In this case, it was Orley's own account of how he could consult the gods and know what was going to happen. English lapped it up like a cat over cream. After that first job, all Orley had to do to survive with this bunch was to tend to English's sense of mysticism. For Orley, that was as easy as falling off his horse.

Sometimes, it was hard for Orley himself to tell

whether he was just making the stuff up or having real visions. As the days had passed since his first visit to the opium dens in San Francisco, things had a way of jumbling up in his mind to the point where it was often hard to tell what was real and what wasn't. So when he consulted the Higher Powers for English, it sometimes seemed like the pictures he was forming in his mind were real. Other times, he just flat made up stories. He learned quickly never to predict a future that had bad news in it. He had done that once, just as a change of pace, and English had sulked and brooded for three days afterward. It took a whale of a new prediction to pull him out of it. After that, all the foretelling was matters that werejust hunky-dory.

There was one hitch in the whole thing. The last couple of predictions had not come true, not even close, and English was growing edgy. The other half of it was that they hadn't hit a town in a week and the bottle of laudanum was down to its last swallow. That meant cramps and terrible headaches and a passel of indescribable miseries, and Orley wasn't so sure as to how much more he could suffer, or how much more the others would suffer his lagging behind. He knew damn certain he had to come up with something big quickly.

The pains hit him in bunches, like needles in his guts, and his head felt like it was going to bust open and his brains would fly out. He reached around and retrieved the bottle out of his saddlebags. Maybe it was the last swallow, but what he was feeling now wasn't worth worrying whether he'd ever get another or not. He drank down what he could get and held onto the bottle like it was a charm and waited for the dreaminess to overtake him. "Something good's going to happen, I can feel it," he sang.

# CHAPTER 11

The five men rode for an hour more and then rested among the rocks and spired buttes of the Badlands Hills. Both men and horses had broken into a sweat under an intense sun. To the distant north, a storm was pushing large, heavy clouds.

The Anger brothers shared a canteen of warm, mossy-tasting water. They tended to stick together and away from the others. Dog found himself a spot on a broad, flat rock and rested there, his hat the only shade. He avoided shady spots like the plague—in country like this, shade could mean snakes. He had been bitten once—a prairie rattler had nipped him on the back of his leg. The leg swelled up like a boiled sausage and hurt like he had stuck it in fire. Snakes were something else he shot on sight.

All three men took notice of Orley riding past them and his struggle to dismount near where English squatted on his heels. Orley plopped down to the ground next to him.

"I'm feeling flumated," he said, half to himself, half to English.

English turned and looked at him as though he were seeing him for the first time.

"I got a vision trying to pop out of my head but the miseries has laid me low. We need to get to a town quick, my medicine is all gone."

"Your dreams have been bad the last two times," responded English.

"You suggesting that maybe I've lost my power to consult the Higher Orders?"

"Things went wrong in Plainview and things went wrong in Cherry Creek."

"Plainview was a celestial mistake," defended Orley. "The stars were not in their proper alignment and we went in a day early because we needed cash—you and the boys insisted. The stars weren't right—we got less than a hundred dollars, but none of us got killed."

"Cherry Creek was a bustout," said English. The way he laid it out was like a challenge.

"I told you later the dream was weak. I was low on my medicine, just like now. And when I get low on my medicine, the dreams are sometimes weak—I don't get to see the whole picture in my head." Orley was starting to sweat and not just from the cramps.

"Cherry Creek was a bustout," English repeated. "There wasn't no bank, there wasn't no store, there wasn't no whiskey tent. There wasn't nothing *to* rob!"

There was only one way Orley knew to defend

himself—and to buy himself some more time with English. "If I don't get the next one right, shoot me!"

"I will," he said seriously.

With his hat dropped down over his eyes, Dog allowed the warmth of the rock to lull him into a light sleep; the shade and the smell of the hat pulled down over his face was a comfort. A dream placed him under a huge apple tree. He was lying on a carpet of grass and above him, hanging from the branches, were bright red apples, smooth as wax. The ground was covered with apples and all he had to do was simply reach out and take one and eat it. He could taste the sweet juices on his tongue and feel the crunch on his teeth. It was a pleasant dream, right up to the time the dead rattlesnake dropped down on his outstretched legs. He came awake with a jolt and the first thing his eyes saw was the rattler.

"God damn!" he yelled as he scrambled out from underneath the dead serpent. The Anger brothers were practically falling all over themselves with delight. They had caught the rattler and brained it with a rock.

The bang of six pistol shots from Dog's .44-caliber Smith & Wesson echoed for a while in the hills. A cloud of smoke veiled the scene: Dog, and the twice-dead rattler that was little more now than a bloody carcass after being chewed up by the slugs.

The sudden volley had caused English to spin around into a crouch from where he had been squatting, his own pistol drawn and ready. Orley had bitten dust and remained there with his hands over the back of his head.

Dog looked from the snake to where the Anger brothers rocked with laughter. The realization that he had been jaked by these two mean sons-a-bitches caused him to lose control of his senses. He pulled the trigger on them but the hammer fell on empty chambers; he had used all his shells up on the snake. Before they knew what hit them, he piled into the two men like a bull, clubbing them with the barrel of his pistol in his right hand, and swinging his other fist like a hammer. They went down in a heap.

Earl caught the first blow of the steel barrel across the bridge of his nose and it made his eyeballs feel like they were boiling in water. Ed took a blow on the side of the head that stunned him for a full five seconds. Earl reached up and grabbed Dog by the throat and was squeezing as hard as he could until Dog laid a second blow to his ear that stung so bad, Earl wasn't sure if his ear hadn't been ripped clear off.

Ed gained his senses back and punched Dog in the ribs three or four times before Dog countered with a knee to Ed's groin which took all the steam out and made him want to cry it hurt so much. Ed was holding onto his nuts like they were leaving to catch the next train out when Dog slammed his fist down on Ed's mouth and nearly knocked him cold. Earl had recovered enough to know that his ear was still attached and that he was in a fight for his life. He brought both hands up and tried to gouge out Dog's eyes with his thumbs. Both men rolled around in the dirt until English's Winchester rifle exploded near their heads.

"You pieces of horseshit, you want to die, I kill you all!" English stood above them, the black maw of the Winchester's octagonal barrel dancing over their faces.

"I got no time for schoolboys. You want to kill each other, go ahead, but you don't ride with me!"

"Well, shit," said Earl Anger, sitting up with his legs spread wide, "we was just funning ol' Dog, is all. He just went plum lunatic over it."

"Ya, that's right," groaned Ed, still holding both hands between his legs. "Hell, we busted that snake's head with a rock, it was as harmless as lace drawers. Go take a look, you don't believe me."

English didn't move the barrel away from their faces.

Dog's eyes went from the black hole of the barrel to the cold stare of English. They didn't have to say it, but they both knew that the next time a gun was drawn between them, someone would die. He moved slow in standing up.

"You keep away from me from now on," he said to the two brothers. "You fool with me again, I'll shoot you in the guts." For all their meanness, there wasn't an ounce of bravery between the two brothers. They sulked like scolded children and nursed their sore spots.

Dog removed himself from the presence of the others and walked off a distance. Right now, all the company he wanted was himself.

Maybe it was time to pack it in, he told himself. It was hell to be a busted-down saddle bum, reduced to riding with half-witted young guns, and cold-blooded killers, and crazy dope fiends. They were mean and dangerous men without honor.

He remembered a time when he had had a wife to come home to and a job that decent folks paid him to do. He remembered a blue-eyed baby daughter who used to follow him around like a kitten and bounce on his knee until they both giggled.

He remembered being loved. He hadn't been loved in a very long time.

How come it had gotten down to robbing people and stealing for a living? he asked himself. Where did his decency ride off and leave him? For a long time, he tried fooling himself with the bottle—liquor had a handsome way of erasing the bad parts. But after a time, the liquor turned on him, too. And like the Anger brothers, and English, he found himself running with the booze as an unwanted partner. They were about the only things that would have him anymore, and even so, time was running out.

He realized he was still holding the Smith & Wesson. He wondered what it might be like—having a .44-caliber slug tear through his skull. He had known men who had done it. Men who had simply run out of things to do with their lives and still found themselves at the bottom of the dung heap in life. In that instant, the urge grew strong as he recalled a voice from the past saying, "Daddy, I love you."

# CHAPTER 12

An hour before dark, Able, Hobe, and Preacher Billy rode into Cold Iron Crossing. It was a burg of not more than a half dozen structures and as many stray dogs trotting the street. The only place that looked alive was a whiskey tent center of town.

"I know you don't drink, Preacher," said Able, "but I think me and Hobe could stand one, and it will give us a chance to ask if Luther rode through here with Annie and any others."

"I'll take the animals down to that blacksmith's and see if I can buy some feed before we start out again," said Bill.

Hobe and Able dismounted and handed their reins to Preacher. "We won't be more than a few minutes, just long enough to swallow a glass and ask questions." Preacher nodded his understanding.

The air inside the tent was close and filled with the smell of men and revealed only what a pair of oil lanterns was able to cast light on: dark, unfriendly faces paying attention to the two strangers. The floor was dirt, and the bar was a board plank resting on two whiskey barrels. A brutish-looking man with forearms the size of piano legs stood behind the bar. He didn't say anything, didn't ask anything, just waited.

"We'll have beer, a glass apiece if you've got it," said Hobe. The man stared at the marshal's badge pinned on Hobe's vest. It seemed like a long time passed with anything getting done. Hobe looked at where the man was staring and then leaned in close to the barkeep's face. "I said, we'll have a beer, one apiece if you got it," he repeated.

"We got no beer," the bartender mumbled.

"Well, then we'll have a whiskey, you got that, don't you?"

Again the man stared down at the badge. "We got no whiskey, neither." Hobe looked around at the other men in the tent.

"Well, if you got no beer, and you got no whiskey, I guess we'll settle for whatever it is them other fellows is drinking."

"Look, mister, you ain't the law here—we ain't got no law here."

Able knew Hobe well enough to know that someone taking offense with him over his position as a lawman was asking for trouble. He interceded.

"Look, friend, we didn't come in here for nothing but a drink and you're making it damn near impossible for us to do that. You didn't hear this man say anything about being the law, did you?"

"He's wearing a badge, he must be after something. Ain't no reason to come in here wearing a badge."

"Well, I'm not taking it off, you son of a bitch!" Hobe reached across the bar and grabbed the man by his shirtfront and yanked him so close they could smell one another's breath. Able covered his play by turning round and watching the dark faces in the tent; his hand rested on the butt of his Colt.

For all his bigness, the man seemed visibly shaken by the suddenness of the assault.

"What's the matter, mister?" Hobe's voice came through his clenched teeth like an angry wind. "You been walking the crooked side of the trail so long that you get all bound up inside at the sight of a badge?" The big man reached for Hobe's wrist and tried to free himself, but the lawman just twisted harder. Only this time, Hobe brought up the long barrel of his Colt and rested the front sight under the bartender's chin.

"Now get a goddamn bottle and set it up here on the bar before I get too pissed off to want to drink it!" He turned loose of the man's shirtfront with a little shove on the end of it. Hobe held his pistol on the man the whole time; it was common to keep a scattergun hidden somewhere. The man rummaged through a wooden case and set a bottle of Old Turkey and two glasses on the board. Hobe poured out a glass for Able and himself and handed Able's around to him. Able took it without turning his back on the others in the tent.

Hobe tossed his drink down and let the liquor burn across his tongue and throat. He recorked the bottle and held onto it. Without taking either his eyes or his pistol off the big man, he asked, "You seen a black man and a white woman and possibly some others ride through here in the last day or so?"

The man knew now not to trifle with an answer. "Ain't seen anybody like that, honest to God!"

Hobe knew he hadn't and there was no use making a bad situation worse by pushing it any further. "How much for the bottle?"

"Take it, you can have it."

"I don't want nothing free from you," said Hobe, full of indignation. "How much for the bottle?"

"Two dollars." And as if to justify the price, "It's the best whiskey in the territory."

Hobe reached in his pocket and found it empty. "Able, you got two dollars on you?" Able produced the money and laid it on the bar. They walked out of the tent, Hobe carrying the bottle, and turned once to look back and see if anybody was following. No one was. They looked at each other, shook their heads and smiled. "Damn meanest place I've been in awhile," said Hobe.

"You should try the Texas Panhandle," said Able.

"Let's go round up Preacher and clear out of this place."

They met up with Preacher Billy halfway down the street. He was holding the reins of the three animals and walking in front.

"You boys have any luck finding out if they seen anyone come through here?" he asked.

"The only one that would talk to us said he hadn't," chuckled Hobe.

"These folks are a little touchy 'round here," said Preacher. "The blacksmith at the livery wanted to charge me ten dollars to water and feed these animals. Can you believe that!"

"Town like this," said Able, "it figures."

"You still believe our quarry is heading for the Badlands, Preacher?" asked Able.

"I don't figure anyplace else they might go. So far, we've been able to pick up their trail whenever they've trotted and allowed that walker to leave his calling card. And so far everything seems to point to that one place a body could lose himself from a posse."

"I'd say we've wasted enough time in this dung pile," said Hobe. "I'm ready to ride."

They swung into their saddles and walked their horses directly down main street and past the whiskey tent where a knot of ugly faces stood watching. "You sure you won't have a taste of this," said Hobe to Preacher holding up the bottle.

"Don't reckon. Look what it did to them."

103

# CHAPTER 13

As Hap led them across the sea of prairie grass, they saw a strange and awesome sight ahead of them. Just beyond the edge of rich grassland with its sprays of chokecherry, silvered leaves of buffalo berry, and pink blossoms of meadow rose, lay the Badlands. Rising out of nowhere, and in the middle of nowhere, it seemed, stood sharp spires, layered buttes, and turrets of rock and mud-colored earth. A land that was tortured and broken by gullies and arroyos.

Hap halted the group with a raised hand. He motioned for Jim to ride up, leaving Lamar holding Annie and Luther at a distance as the two men walked their horses out of earshot.

"Once we get inside that place, Jim Buck, I want you to stay behind with Luther. Give us about an hour to get gone and then you dust him good."

Jim studied the landscape ahead of them for a long minute. "You care to tell me how I'm supposed to find you in that mess if I give you an hour's lead time?" Consternation had screwed up Jim Buck's face.

Hap studied the land too and finally pointed to a single spire that stood up like a long, gray thumb. "We'll ride to the base of that and wait for you."

Hap started to spur his mount back toward the others when Jim Buck motioned for him to wait. "I been thinking on something," he said, allowing his horse to crop some of the rich grass.

"What's stuck in your craw?"

"How is it that me and Lamar wind up getting the same share when it's me doing all the killing?"

"Well, for one thing, I thought we had an agreement." Hap tried hard to conceal his irritation at Jim Buck's questioning of his authority to cut the pie any way he wanted to. As far as he was concerned, Jim Buck was just a hired gun, nothing more. But on the other hand, he knew the man to be a killer tried and true, and if he was going to maintain control over him, it was going to have to be with guile, not with a direct challenge.

"For the other thing," continued Hap, "I figured you liked that part of it. But if you want, I'll have Lamar do the killing from now on. Trouble is, I don't know if he can handle it—he ain't the brightest star to shine in the sky."

"Well, I just don't cut it as equal. From here on, you want someone shot, you pay me extra."

*The damn fool,* Hap thought to himself. *What he*

*don't know is if everything works out as planned,
I won't need to pay anybody anything, especially
two peckerwoods like him and Lamar.*

"How much you want for plying your trade this
time, Jim?" Jim Buck seemed surprised at how
easy the negotiation had gone. It took him a few
seconds to come up with a price.

"A hundred dollars a man!" he blurted, hoping
he could sneak that one by Hap as easily as he
had his first argument.

"A hundred dollars?" repeated Hap. "Jim, I
never figured you for a businessman, but I can
see I misjudged you right from the start. A
hundred dollars a man it is." Hap threw in a
little laugh to let Jim know he appreciated being
outfoxed on the deal.

Luther Pride watched as the two men palavered in
the distance. He saw Jim Buck turn and look back
at him long enough to send a chill up his backside. He had fought white boys in the war, and he
had been a buffalo soldier, and he had learned
enough about the way men were to stay alive this
long. He knew the two men were planning on
killing him. He tested the strength of the strip of
rawhide tied around his wrists, his hands nearly
numb from it.

*It only makes sense they kill you, boy. You the
one going to be blamed for the robbery and
kidnapping Miss Annie. They going to kill you*

*and leave you hid up in those rocks somewheres.*
The conversation ran through his head like
rainwater running off a roof. *And if you was
lucky enough to get gone from these blue-eyed
devils, what you think a posse of white men
going to do to you if they catch you? Hanging
might not be the worst of it.*

In the war, at nineteen years old, death used to
be nothing to him. He had survived so many
border skirmishes against tough Rebel boys that
he got used to paying no more attention to death
than he would to crows sitting on a fence. And
when the war ended, he thought he was free
from all the killing, but he never was.

The war proved to be no worse than peacetime
in a whole lot of ways. Coming home a soldier
didn't prove a thing; white men still controlled
most everything, and to them, he was just a
no-account lowlife because he was black.

Leastways in the army, in a black regiment, he
was equal to the others. And when they fought at
Cabin Creek and Honey Springs and a dozen
other places in the Indian Territory, the white
commanders held them in high regard. Sometimes the fighting was so fierce and close, there
wasn't room for shooting. It was bayonets, and
choking a man's life out with your bare hands, or
crushing in his skull with the butt of your rifle.
And sometimes at night, so much death lay on the
battlefield that the ghosts of men returned,

keening on the wind, and blew the stink of your work up so's you could smell it for days after.

He tried not to remember that part of it, but he did.

Ultimately, the white man's peace proved more difficult than his war. The only good thing to come out of that time between the wars he fought in was Dahlia Rose. A sweeter woman there never was, with skin the color of creamed coffee and almond eyes that could look right into his heart.

He had come across her in Wichita—just one more place he had drifted to after the war. Being too long in the saddle had left him in need of companionship by the time he rode down the broad, dusty streets of that community. He learned quickly enough where the colored whores worked their trade—a row of cribs east of town.

The brothel was run by a high-toned woman who called herself Big Momma Cotton. And big she was. Three hundred pounds of bustle and smiles, and how-do's to every peckerwood that strode through her doorway.

Outside was painted fresh white so it looked like a big pearl among the shanties, and tents all around it. Inside was like walking into a palace. Red velvet drapes hung from every window, and the furniture was all French this and Italian that. There were rugs from Persia lying on the floors, and in one room, there was a tiger-skin rug with the head still on it, lying in front of a fireplace big enough to stand in.

Big Momma Cotton had greeted him at the front door wearing a blue satin dress, as hot as it was outside, and a smile that flashed a row of teeth white as a picket fence. She had looked at him a long time before she allowed him to step inside.

"I can see you are not from around here," she said with a certain air about her.

"How do you know that?" Luther asked.

"Your clothes is better'n most," and looking down at his feet, "there's no town colored I know that wears new calfskin boots like those."

Luther quickly grew impatient, he hadn't come here to discuss where he was from or what he was wearing. "I hear tell this is the best colored whorehouse in Kansas, that true?"

"Honey, this is the best whorehouse west of the Mississippi, colored or white!"

"Well, do you take customers or don't you?"

"We do indeed," she laughed aloud. "But baby, you can't be coming in Big Momma Cotton's all covered with dust like you is."

"So you telling me I'm not good enough to buy one of your whores?" Luther's pride was beginning to smart. It was one thing for the white man to keep you out, but for a colored woman to turn you away from her whorehouse. . . .

"No honey, you are good enough to buy anything you want, providing you got the money. But what you got to do first is take yourself a bath and freshen up them clothes—you smell like horses, or worse. You go around back and I'll have Dahlia Rose heat you up some bath water—we've got a bath tub all the way from New Jersey. And while you're washing up, she can beat the dust out of them clothes you're wearing. Afterwards, you come into the parlor, walk right through the kitchen, and pick out any girl you want—or any two if you got a big enough hunger." When she laughed, her eyes glimmered like wet stones.

That's how he first met Dahlia Rose. She was as shy as a preacher's child. She hardly spoke a word. His eyes never left her. He watched as she came in and out of the room with the buckets of water she brought from the kitchen. She seemed too frail to even carry them, but she did fine. And she picked his clothes up, took them out back, cleaned them properly, and laid them out on a chair as neatly as if he were going to get married in them.

Everything about her endeared her to him, the way she walked and looked and kept quiet. And when he finished his bath and stood up naked in front of her, she didn't flinch, but simply took soft towels and dried his skin.

He paid Big Momma Cotton for her. And for the first time ever, Luther Pride found himself being gentle with a woman. He felt a contentment and peace with her. And for the first time, he allowed a woman to hold him in her arms and let the past wash down his cheeks and not feel ashamed for doing so.

# CHAPTER 14

Luther's reverie was broken by the sight of the two men riding back toward him and the others. He saw too, the way Jim Buck never took his eyes off of him the whole way. In that instant, Luther made up his mind he wasn't going to let this man kill him easily.

The lot of them followed Hap Patterson's lead toward the stretch of Badlands that lay before them. Once they crossed over into it, the land seemed to swallow them up, everything looked different and the same, all at once.

In a short while, they reached a place where the ground was gashed by a deep arroyo. Hap halted their procession. "We're going to split up here," he said as though it was something that had just come to him. "Annie, you and me and Lamar are going off one way. Jim Buck and your colored are going off another—that's so if anyone's following, they won't have a single trail to go after. We'll all meet up later." It was obvious to Luther that this whole speech was for Annie's benefit. Hap didn't want a hysterical woman on his hands, and he wasn't about to kill his own sister.

Jim Buck nudged his horse alongside Luther's. "Hold on, boy. You and me are going to wait here awhile," he ordered.

Luther saw Annie look back at them as they started off, but Hap grabbed the reins of her walker and quickly led it down the arroyo; the fat man followed, and they were gone. They sat there a long time, Luther and Jim Buck.

Jim Buck pulled some makings out of his shirt pocket and rolled himself a cigarette and smoked it slow, letting the smoke curl back into his nose.

"You can get down off your horse now," he ordered Luther after he was nearly through smoking his cigarette. "You won't have no more use for horses where you're going."

Luther let his mind run hard. There wasn't much to keep him alive except his own wit; he needed to divert Jim Buck's focus, even for a split instant.

"You going to shoot me in the back," he said sarcastically. "Man like you looks like he might be a back shooter."

He could see the cold smirk on Jim Buck's face change ever so slightly at the remarks.

"You know how much I'm getting paid to kill you, nigger? A hundred dollars. Can you believe that? I got Hap to pay me a hundred dollars to blow your goddamn head off. Hell, I was gonna do it for free, just like I shot that sum-a-bitch banker!"

Luther had slid out of the saddle the whole time Jim Buck was talking. He allowed his bound wrists and hands to rest on the saddle horn. He was thinking of after the war, later when he couldn't stand peace anymore and joined up to fight Indians as a buffalo soldier. The war had taught him how to kill and how to be scared sometimes and how to anticipate your enemy. White people were mostly predictable, even in war. But fighting Indians, now that was a different piece of cake altogether. Fighting Indians taught you how to survive, if you paid attention.

"You look like the man whose mama I once paid a dollar to bed me," Luther said, hoping to bait him. It worked.

Jim Buck jerked his pistol out of its holster with such a start his horse wheeled round. It was enough. Luther grabbed the rein and held onto the saddle horn at the same instant he brought his horse between Jim Buck and him; four years in the cavalry had taught him how to handle a horse in the worst conditions.

"You got some smart mouth on you!" he heard Jim Buck yell. Using rein and body, he charged the horse toward the still-mounted enemy. He heard the roar of Jim Buck's big Remington and the scream of his horse as the slug tore through the animal's neck. But his own tremendous strength and skill allowed him to control the horse long enough to send it crashing into that of Jim Buck's.

The impact knocked Jim Buck's mount over backwards, landing on top of the gunman. Twelve hundred pounds of horse crashed down on the rider, shattering his pelvis, busting ribs, and knocking all the air out of his lungs so that his screams were little more than short, hard gasps.

Luther had flung himself free just before the impact and now scrambled to his feet. His own horse lay kicking and screaming, a geyser of blood spraying from its neck. Jim Buck's horse managed to stand, but its right front foreleg was obviously broken as it tried to take steps.

For several long moments, all Jim Buck could see was a blue sky with clouds the size of sailing ships gathering overhead. He fought for air by tossing his head from side to side and he could feel nothing but pain coming up from everywhere. He wanted to sit up and breathe, but he could not. Then a shadow fell over him—a dusty black man's shadow.

"You're dying, mister," was all the shadow said. Luther could see Jim Buck staring at him as if he were some sort of apparition. For a long few minutes they were like that, Jim Buck lying on the ground and Luther Pride standing over him. Finally, Jim Buck was able to draw enough breath into the lungs that were being tortured by the broken ribs.

"How could some no-account nigger get me down this-a-way?" he said in a harsh whisper.

Luther had seen before, what hate could do to men and where it could take them, but he didn't reckon he'd ever met a man with as much hate and meanness as Jim Buck.

"How you're dying," he said finally, "ain't no good way to go. I seen it lots when I was in the cavalry. A horse-crushed man can linger for hours, even days afore he dies. It's terrible."

Jim Buck's eyes fixed on Luther's the way a trapped animal will stare at its captor. "How I'm dying ain't none of your concern!" A trickle of blood that had been dribbling from the corner of his mouth flecked his chin as he spat the words with all the anger he had in him.

"Naw, you see, that's where you got it all wrong," said Luther. "How you're dying is my concern. That man you kilt, Miss Annie's husband, he was a good man, a Christian man. Hired me when I didn't have nothing, gave me a place to live, and work to do. I don't believe it would be the Christian thing to do to just stand here and let a man suffer like you surely must be right now."

Jim Buck saw the barrel of his big Remington appear in the hands of Luther Pride. Before his mind could register the roar, the bullet tore through his brain and released him from his suffering.

Luther undid the dead man's gun belt and buckled it around his own waist. He felt little compassion for the man he had killed. He walked over to the injured horse and placed the barrel of the Remington to its forehead and pulled the trigger once more. There wasn't any easy way to kill a horse, and that he did feel bad about. He undid the half-full canteen that had been looped around the saddle horn and sat down and took a long drink of it. Warm as the water had become, it tasted like ambrosia.

He closed his eyes against the carnage that lay all around him. His own horse had long since breathed its last, and blood from the three dead bodies was turning the ground red.

As he sat and rested, he allowed his mind to drift back to Dahlia Rose again. He remembered that first time with her and how it had felt to be delicate with someone, and how afterwards, she lay there sleeping in his arms, and she smelled like lilacs. He remembered being happy.

He courted her for nearly two weeks, then talked her into marrying him and giving up "the life." She was like a little girl with a week of birthdays over the proposal. They lived in a tent two miles out of town until he could build a soddy, and it was the first real home either of them ever had.

He could see her there now, standing in the doorway of that soddy with the grass growing up on the roof, and her smiling as he worked a small patch of garden trying to get some damned carrots and cabbages to grow, which he never did because the rabbits came and ate them.

Before he opened his eyes he was hoping that what he was seeing was where he was, but it wasn't. The dead man and the dead horses still lay around him, and the buzz of flies hummed in the still air as they feasted on the wounds of the dead.

To hell with this, he told himself. He took another swallow of the water and allowed himself a few more minutes of dreaming about her.

The warm nights of lying in that house and loving his Dahlia Rose was as near to all-around happiness as he had ever known. Sometimes they'd even lie out on a quilt under the stars and stare up at what she called "a sky full of diamonds," and watch for shooting stars and look for the face of the man in the moon.

But ultimately, Wichita proved no better a place for a black man getting good work than others he had been. And spring turned to summer and the heat and the rain took turns at turning the soddy into a miserable place to be cooped up in all day and night. And despite how much they loved one another, Luther grew restless and Dahlia grew dispirited.

At best, his trips to town to look for work ended

with him working for drinks and listening to the latest news about how the Plains Indians were raising hell and how the army was looking for fighters to take the hellions on. Luther maybe wasn't the best husband or the best provider, he admitted to himself, but he was a damn good fighter. Maybe that was the only thing he was good at.

He remembered how she cried for a long time when he told her he was going to join the army again. "What you expect me to do, woman, sit around here and watch my garden get eaten by rodents?"

"What am I going to do?" she asked. "I can't follow you, and I can't live out here alone." He realized the implication of her plea. It was true. A black woman alone . . . The thought of her going back to Big Momma Cotton's was like having a knife stuck in his guts. But he didn't see any other way around it for her either.

He packed up her things and rode her into Wichita on the back of his horse and left her on Big Momma Cotton's doorstep. He rode to the nearest army post and signed up to fight Indians, which he did plenty of in the Ninth Cavalry regiment for the next three years.

And now he found himself sitting in this awful place with three more dollops of death dropped on him. There wasn't any army and there wasn't any Dahlia Rose, and there wasn't even a reason in the whole world he should be sitting here. At least, none he could think of.

"Maybe I should of stayed with Dahlia and raised me up some babies," he said to himself. The flies buzzed. Maybe so.

He stood up, stuck the big Remington inside his belt, took the half-filled canteen in hand, and started off in the direction they had come from the last three days. It was a risk, heading back. But not as risky as going a way he knew nothing about.

# CHAPTER 15

Hap Patterson halted the run he had begun across the broken land in order to let the horses catch their breath. He wanted to press on, to lose the trail he had promised Jim Buck they'd take. One less split of the pie would do nicely, but he had to make sure that Jim Buck would not catch up to them first. He scoured the landscape all around them; the land was so sore and twisted, it didn't seem possible anyone could find them, even by accident. But still, Hap did not want to take any chances that Jim Buck would come up on them.

He looked back at his sister, her face caked with dirt and streaked from crying. He felt sorry for her in that moment but there was not a whole lot he could or would do about it.

She saw him watching her and she hated him. She had never felt hatred for anyone before this ordeal began. He had ceased being kin to her the night he robbed Ben's bank. Now he was just another badman taking advantage of anyone he could. She wondered what made men that way. The times were full of men like Hap Patterson, and Jim Buck, and Lamar. She saw them every

121

time she had gone into Deadwood. Men who lounged on the streets in their dirty clothes and watched you with hollow eyes, and spoke in whispers to one another as you passed by them. Men who would kill you, or worse, given half the chance. Some were tough, some were weak, some were stupid, all were mean. Mean men in a mean land.

"I got to get down off this-here hoss," said Lamar, his face bunched up in a petulant pout. "My butt's as sore as raw bacon." Hap did not argue that point. The fat man nearly fell trying to get out of the saddle, then walked around rubbing his backside with both hands and saying, "Whew-ee!"

"Lamar, you come help Annie down off her horse," he ordered.

"Yessir!" Lamar relished the idea of being near the woman. Annie was too weary to resist the large hands reaching up and grasping her by the waist. She felt herself being lifted clear of the saddle and gently lowered to the ground. She found herself looking up into the porcine face with its beady eyes—eyes that looked like they were devouring her—eyes that made her skin crawl. She waited for him to remove his thick hands from around her waist. She could feel the hot dampness of his fleshy fingers coming though the dirty gingham dress she was wearing. She waited. He just stood there, mouth half-open like a sprung gate.

"You can leave her be now," said Hap, noticing the delay. "Annie, I'd guess you need a few moments of privacy—there's some tall rocks over there if you need to relieve yourself. We ain't staying here longer than it takes for the horses to cool down, and we ain't stopping again until we have to."

Hap swung down from the saddle and stretched his legs. He felt nature's call but he didn't want to walk off and leave Annie alone with Lamar. "Come on, Lamar. Let's me and you go wet down some of those rocks over there. Let's leave Annie some privacy. "

Lamar looked befuddled at the comment. He really didn't want to go too far away from her now that he had had the chance to touch her and feel the weight of her in his hands; soft and light as a newborn calf, she was. Finally he released her and she backed away from him in short stumbling steps.

"You go on now, Miss Annie. I'll go with Hap, you go on and pee if you have to," he said to her as though there was something significant about the moment and he had just approved it.

She wasn't aware that she was going to say anything, it just came out in a half scream, half curse: "You bastards! You mean, stupid bastards!" Her anger choked off her words as she stood there facing them, her fists clenched at her sides. She wanted to kill them. Lamar looked as though he had just been stung in the face by a whip. He stammered something inaudible and then dropped his head like a scolded schoolboy so that the only thing he had to look at was the toes of his new shoes.

Hap avoided looking at her directly but instead looked at the fat man. "Annie, I don't think ol' Lamar meant any indignities toward you. He was just meaning to be a help, weren't you Lamar?" He hoped the fool had enough brains to apologize. They were still a hell of a ways from the Nebraska Territory. Once there, he'd send Annie back home, and rid himself of Lamar. Until that time, he had to keep a lid on things. Lamar stood silent as a sphinx.

"Lamar, you hear me? I said to apologize to Annie."

"He doesn't need to say anything!" She had fought down her anger enough to speak again. "Neither of you has to speak to me again. Hap, why are you doing this to me? You've got what you want, can't you just leave me and ride off?"

"Annie, if I was to leave you here by yourself, it would be the same as me taking a gun and shooting you. You wouldn't last a day. Just hold on until we get to Nebraska Territory. You do that, I'll see you get back home safe and sound. I promise!"

"Your word's no good, Hap Patterson. You are a thief and a liar, and anything you tell me, I will

124

not believe. I would as soon be dead as to take one more step with you or this man." She charged at him, flailing her arms and fists and struck him sharp, stinging blows to his face and neck. He grabbed her wrists but she tore free and continued to hit him. He shoved her away but she was so filled with anger that she sprang at him again. He felt his own anger rising at her attack. "Goddammit, Annie, stop it before I . . ."

"Before you what? she screeched, her nails digging at his face.

Without thinking, he brought the back of his hand up in an arc and struck her across the side of her cheek, snapping her head back and causing her to drop to her knees. Her right hand still clung to his shirtfront and her falling almost toppled him over on top of her. He grabbed her wrist and tried to twist free. Blood trickled from the side of her mouth and a red welt was forming high on her cheekbone. She struggled to regain her feet and he pushed her back down again. She screamed and kicked and clawed at him and he was at a loss to control her. She cursed him. He brought his fist down at a sharp, hard angle against her jaw and she fell away from him.

He was breathing hard when the weight of the fat man landed on his back and knocked him to his hands and knees. He tried to twist out from under the bulk that was pinning him down but it was useless.

"You're goin' to stop hurtin' her!" Lamar said.

Hap managed to get half-twisted around until he was looking directly up into the fat man's rage-darkened face. The son of a bitch was defending Annie's honor! He didn't have enough brains to come in out of the rain, and he was defending her honor! Hap tried desperately to free his right arm and reach his pistol. His surprise at the attack had turned to anger: He'd blow holes in this lardbelly—shoot him until his guts spilled out.

But Lamar had his knees pressing down hard on Hap's arms, and the pistol had been knocked free and was lying several feet from the struggling men.

"Get off me, Lamar! What the hell are you doing, anyway?" The press of the big man's weight was making it difficult for Hap to breathe. "Look . . . Lamar, I wasn't trying to hurt her . . . she's my own kin . . . why would I try to hurt her?"

Lamar glared down at him, his eyes wildly bulging in the fat purple face, his weight crushing. Hap felt a sudden shift in Lamar's weight, enough for him to gasp breath. He used every ounce of strength that was in him to dislodge the big man from his chest, but once again, Lamar had shifted his weight directly atop his victim.

Through the blinding glare of an overhead sun, Hap glimpsed something big and round in

Lamar's hands. He saw Lamar lift the rock high above his head, blotting out the sun. A cold fear rushed through him as Lamar brought the rock down hard and fast on Hap Patterson's face. The impact made a dull smacking sound when it struck flesh and bone, crushing the front part of Hap's skull.

Three more times Lamar lifted the rock and brought it down.

Annie had regained her senses just as Lamar brought the rock down for the final time. She saw Hap's blood on the rock and tried desperately to choke down the nausea that was clogging her throat, but couldn't. Lamar looked up from his study of the dead man beneath him at the sound of Annie's retching. Through the sting of tears, she saw him coming toward her. Although the pistol lay on the ground a few feet away from her, it made no difference because the violence had overwhelmed her to the point of leaving her helpless.

She wanted to run but had no strength left in her to move. Instead, she stayed there on the ground, on her hands and knees, waiting for him to kill her too.

He moved slowly, as if he were wading through water. Little rivulets of mucous ran from his nostrils; his shirt was blotched with dark spots of his sweat and Hap's blood.

Annie waited—death would be a relief.

# CHAPTER 16

They had pushed it as far as they could before making camp that night. Neither Able Guthrie nor Hobe Waters had ever come this way before, so it was difficult to imagine this gentle sweep of land turning into Badlands the way Preacher Bill described it.

They had hobbled their horses and laid out their bedrolls near the small fire they had built. The flames licked at the night as though trying to drink up the darkness. The sky was blanketed with so many stars that parts of it looked like it had been sprayed with milk; the clear night brought with it a hard chill—the fire was small relief.

Preacher Bill went over to his saddlebags and pulled out a poke and carried it back to the fire.

"Boys, it ain't much to sustain three weary buckaroos, but it is all that I have to offer." He squatted down between the other two men. He reached into the sack and pulled out three powdered biscuits the size of bullfrogs and a Ball jar of peach preserves.

"I got some others in here, along with some beef jerky and hardtack, but I figure we better ration them as we go along. Here, help your-selves—they're Inge's specialty. Ain't much with-out some preserves on them, but I never told her that. It would break her heart—took her a month just to learn how to make 'em so's they wouldn't break your toe if you dropped one on it. The preserves, I made." He smiled like a gassy baby.

The three shared the biscuits all around, smearing them with big gobs of peach preserves and licking off their fingers what missed the biscuits. It wasn't much, that was true, but it chased the hungries off some. They hadn't taken much when they set out, and game had been scarce as bald-headed women ever since they left Deadwood.

Still tasting the sweetness of the jam and feeling the warmth of fire, Able felt the sense a man gets being alone with his pards, like they were the only three people left on earth. He realized in that moment that he had not been very congenial ever since this whole affair had started. He had been so caught up in his concern for Annie that he had all but ignored their part in getting this far. He could just as easily have been sitting out here alone, maybe still pushing himself on out into the darkness, letting his anger and fear override any sense he'd ever had. He realized too, that without Hobe and Preacher Bill along, his chances of finding Annie were slim to none—at least, finding her alive. And as his eyes drifted to the two men across the fire from him, he knew that they had allowed him to stay inside himself.

"Boys, I need to set something right between us," he began. Hobe and Preacher stared into the fire. They weren't looking for an apology and it made them feel stiff hearing one coming.

"My personal need to get Annie back has stepped all over my appreciation for what you two are doing to help me." Able paused for a long moment before continuing. "A man likes to believe he can do anything he sets his mind to, set any wrong right—protect the people he loves. It ain't always so. And when a man realizes he can't do things that he feels he must, it's worse than being whipped. That's what happened to me the minute Hobe broke the news." He paused again and swallowed.

"I most likely would have caught whoever was responsible for what was done, but it might have been a long time—too long a time to save Annie. Truth is, I still love her the same as when we were married, the same as I always have. I never stopped, even after she married Ben.

"When I came back to Deadwood the first time, it was because I heard she was living there. We wound up spending time together. I'm not proud of the way we had to do it, it wasn't right, but it didn't seem like neither of us could control it at the time. I guess down deep, I still felt like she was *my* wife. It didn't seem to matter to me that she wasn't. Now Ben's dead and I feel sorry as hell about that, it was like I somehow helped kill him. I knew Annie loved him too, we had both pretty much agreed we couldn't keep it up—we're not that kind of people.

"I took the job of bringing Charley Justice back because I wanted the money to head south to Arizona, buy a place, and try to find some peace with myself." He stopped talking for a minute and examined the sky as though the rest of his words were up there.

"You know, awhile before his death Judge Nevers as much as told me his wife was unfaithful. I couldn't understand why he'd still want a woman who would run around with another man. I can now. He loved her and that was all that mattered to him. You boys have my thanks." Able allowed his gaze to fall from the sky to the glowing coals of the fire.

Hobe had known Able Guthrie for nearly ten years and would have bet wages that he'd never hear what he'd just heard. Able was not the silent type, like some men; neither was he a man who talked a lot about his feelings. Hobe studied his friend as he sat there by the fire, light and shadow playing off the tall figure.

Able's hair was thinner, the limp more noticeable at times, the face more creased maybe, around the eyes especially. But in Hobe's view, Able Guthrie was still more man than most he could name. He still had that lean toughness of men who had got that way during the war and never settled down long enough afterward to grow fat and weak. And though he had not seen Able in a fight in a long time, he remembered a man whose fists could be like hammers in driving a man down.

Hobe remembered too, that while Able wasn't always the most accurate shot—Curly Bill held that honor among the three—he was fearless in a gunfight. Usually, while the other fellow was banging away, Able would simply take his time, aim at the big part of the man, and hit him somewhere good enough to put an end to it.

One time Able had gotten into it with a shootist out of east Texas, a man named Mudlow. It had started like most fights, practically out of nothing. A word said loosely, and offense taken; more words, then a challenge laid down; a challenge taken up. The man had talked tough, said he was a shootist and would dust Able, front and back, and that Able might just as well make peace with whatever God he believed in, for he wouldn't have any other chance later. Hobe had to smile at remembering it. Able listened to the fellow about a half a minute, and the man was still talking when Able pulled his pistol out and aimed it at the shootist. He recalled Able saying, "Mister, the biggest favor I could do anybody is to shoot your tongue off."

Mudlow pulled his own gun and started popping off shells. Able shot him through the kidneys, claiming later he had been aiming only to wound the man. "I don't enjoy killing any man," Able had said. "There are some men that deserve it, but not many. It's better if you have to shoot someone to just bang them up good enough for them to remember what it feels like, most won't have nothing more to do with gunfighting if they've been shot in the right places."

Now Preacher spoke, responding to Able's thank-you. "Able, you were not obliged to tell us what's in your heart, or your mind. I can't speak for Hobe, but I believe what we're doing, we're doing because it is the better thing to do. What went on between you and Annie is something nobody can work out but the two of you. As a preacher, I'd call it wrong: as a man, I can understand it. I don't think there is a one of us that hasn't been somewhere we wished now we'd never had gone to, but in my book that just means we're all human."

Preacher paused long enough to rub his hands over what little heat remained from the dying fire. "Able, I got me a wife and babies waiting back home. Inge cried when I left, I knew she would before I told her. It's a hard thing, seeing a woman crying over you. But there is a greater thing going on here than leaving some folks behind and going after others. The Bible says,

'Faith without works is no faith at all.' You coming and asking me was nothing more than giving me a chance to live my faith. It's me that ought to be thanking you."

"I appreciate your sentiments, Preacher, I truly do."

"Well, hell, I guess Preacher speaks for both of us," said Hobe. "As long as we're passing the truth around, maybe you ought to know, Able, that your feelings for Annie were as plain as the ears on an elephant, at least to me. I don't think Ben ever knew, and now it'd make no difference. Annie was always a favorite of mine, and I'd have come out here for her sake even if you wasn't around." He looked directly into the pale gray eyes of his friend. "It seems clear enough that we're all three here because we chose to be. I guess that's all that any of us have to say."

Able saw Hobe's solid face in the dimming light, saw the sincerity in it, and felt glad to call Hobe his friend.

Somewhere in the distant night, wolves called back and forth.

The same night that descended on the three trackers had closed in on a single figure crossing the landscape on foot, a half-full canteen and a Remington pistol his only comforts against the cold, black night. Occasionally he would look up at the quarter moon and see the smoke of clouds passing across it; it was going to rain before morning, he knew that much. *The stars shine cold, and the clouds'll bring rain, Lord, Lord!*

Luther had been walking since midday, walking back to God knows where, but somewhere. He had been careful to keep a lookout for anyone at all. Especially anyone who might be a posseman. He couldn't allow himself to get caught before he got back to Deadwood. Knowing the way things were bound to look, a posse would most likely murder him on the spot. He had determined that once he made it back, he would turn himself in to Marshal Hobe Waters. He didn't know much about the lawman, other than that he had heard he was fair and took his job seriously; there didn't seem to be any other real choice if he was to get some help for Annie and clear his own name.

*Lord, if I was a praying man, which I ain't really, I'd be praying for a good horse and a plate of hot beans along with a beefsteak plopped down in the middle of them.* Holding a conversation in his head was the only way to pass the endless time of walking.

*And after that, I'd wish I was sleeping in a warm bed somewheres where there ain't nothing but black folks living, and me the mayor of the whole lot. And finally, I'd be wanting for Dahlia Rose to be laying in that nice warm bed alongside me.* It felt like a long time until daybreak.

# CHAPTER 17

He stood there for a long time, she could hear him breathing heavily. She was no longer afraid. She was prepared for whatever would happen.

He looked at her with dull, unaffected eyes. "Miss?"

She did not answer.

"I . . ." He raised his bloody hands in an effort to explain what his thoughts could not. "He's dead. I stopped him."

She felt herself becoming sick.

"He shouldn't of . . ."

She glared at the bumbling man in front of her. "Please, don't say any more!"

He shook his head and took a step toward her. She stepped back. He reached one hand to touch her.

"I don't mean you harm, miss." His hand patted her hair slightly as though he were petting an animal. She realized in that moment that he had no intention of hurting her. He had killed Hap out of a sense of wanting to protect her, even though he had helped in her abduction.

She brushed his hand away from her hair.

"Please, don't do that." He let his arm drop to his side but did not step back away from her. She rushed to gather her thoughts; survival was possible if she kept her wits about her.

"We have to leave this place, miss," he told her. He once again reached for her but she withdrew.

"Let me go. Take the money and let me go . . . I won't tell on you."

"We have to leave this place," he repeated.

"To go where?"

"I don't know, exactly. But this is a bad place."

He spoke to her like a child afraid of the dark—it gave her hope. He had killed for her; what else might he do if she asked him, if she talked to him in a way that he could understand?

"Lamar—that is your name?" He nodded that it was. "Lamar, I need to get home again. My husband will be worried about me. . . ." She saw a change in his eyes when she mentioned Ben, but she continued. "I know you just went along with what the others wanted you to do. I'll tell anyone who asks that you had no hand in wanting this to happen. You help me to get home, and I'll make sure that no one does anything to you."

He shook his head. "I can't do that. They'll blame me for what we did back there."

"No! I won't let them! I'll tell them that you helped rescue me—which will be true if you take me home."

He grew agitated and shuffled his feet and wiped his nose on his sleeve.

"I can't!"

"But why not?"

"Because of Jim Buck killin' yore husband like he done! Said he made him kneel down like he was praying and then shot him in the head. They'll hang me for certain—I'm the one that'll catch blame for it!"

Her first instinct was not to believe what he had just told her, although she had feared as much. At least before now she had been able to hope Hap had told her the truth about Ben's safety.

She choked back her anger and pain. She must survive, if nothing more than to see this killer brought to a final justice. And the one left behind with Luther.

She swallowed hard and found her voice. "If you will help me to return home, I will tell the truth and that you did not have a hand in killing Ben. You weren't there when Ben was killed, so no one can accuse you of murder as long as I'm there to tell them what happened. If you don't help me get back, I can't help *you*. Do you understand?"

He looked down at her, the breath audible through his nostrils. "I'd still be scared they would, though," he said, rubbing one hand against his hip. She knew that he would not take her back to Deadwood.

"Where would you take me then, if not home? We can't stay here in this land with nothing to eat, no water to drink."

"Mud Butte! I got a daddy in Mud Butte! We could go there!"

"Which way is Mud Butte, Lamar?"

He turned, looking in several directions. "I think it's back toward that way," he said, pointing off toward the north. "Back the way we came down from."

She was relieved that he did not realize they would be heading for Deadwood.

"Lamar, I think that we should go to Mud Butte, go to where your daddy lives. I think that would be a good place for us to go." She did not yet know how or when she would escape from him, but once they were clear of the Badlands, she would find a way.

He grinned at the proposal. He thought she was the most beautiful creature he had ever seen. Just standing this close to her made him feel funny. He was glad he had killed Hap Patterson. He would kill any man that tried to bring harm to her. He'd ride her home and show her to his daddy—keep her there with them.

"I'll do it, miss. My pap would sit up and take notice, I was to bring home a gal like you. I bet a good dollar, he ain't never seen anyone so handsome as you." She read his thoughts and would suffer his delusions for as long as it would serve her purpose. But she knew, too, that she must not lead him beyond a point—he was still a dangerous man.

Suddenly, he diverted his attention away from her. He squealed with excitement. "Lordy, I near forgot about all the money we robbed out of that bank. I guess it's ours now. Wait till my pap sees all that money—he'll have a conniption!"

"Yes, your daddy will be proud of you, Lamar. The sooner we get started, the sooner your pap will see how well you've done for yourself."

He paused in his jubilation and stared at her in an odd way. She was anxious to get started north. She waited impatiently for him to say what was on his mind. Finally, after what seemed several minutes, she asked, "What is the trouble, Lamar?"

He moved within inches of her, she could smell his sourness, but she did not flinch.

"I was thinkin'," he said, his eyes now narrowed. "You don't no longer have a man."

The words stabbed her heart, but she remained silent.

"It just seems right for a woman to have her a man," he continued. "I ain't got no woman myself—never have had one. Maybe when we get to my pap's place, you could be my woman— maybe we could get married!"

She eyed the pistol that lay not far from Hap's body. If only she could reach it, this thing would end, here and now. But she had to be careful. She had already witnessed the strength of his wrath against Hap.

"We got plenty of money to live on," he said. "Enough so's we wouldn't have to live with my pap if we didn't want to."

"Lamar, what you say makes good sense." If only she could make the promise seem true, even for a little while, it would purchase her a chance to escape. "You must promise me something."

"Anything. Anything at all."

"You must promise me, that until we are married, you will not be improper with me in any way. Do you know what that means?"

"I sorta do."

"You must make that promise to me here and now, or I won't go with you. You must not touch me or harm me in any way. Do you promise me that?"

"I do. Not until our wedding day."

She had no choice but to believe him. "Good. I think that we should get started very quickly, it will be dark soon." She turned and walked toward where the horses were. She felt weary and each step was a labor. But she knew that each step brought her closer to the end of this ordeal.

She reached the walker and placed one hand on the saddle horn before turning back to take a final look at the body of the man who had been her brother. She felt no true sorrow for him, but she

141

was sorry she could not pick up his gun without Lamar noticing.

She pulled herself into the saddle. Lamar had made a feeble effort to assist her, but she managed to elude his touch. The walker pranced nervously and she considered for one brief instant the thought of digging her heels into his side and letting him have his head. But where would she go? And if it proved that she could not outrun Lamar, then she would have given away her only hope of manipulating him to help her toward freedom, and a final justice for Ben. She held the horse steady and waited for the fat man to get mounted.

He had gathered up the reins to Hap's sorrel, preferring that animal over his own. The grain sacks of money were tied to its saddle. He led it over toward where she sat. Something split the air with a bang!

A puff of dust spanked the front of Lamar's shirt. Surprise registered on his face. He dropped the reins of the sorrel and took two short steps backward. His mouth worked open and closed as if he were trying to get out words that were stuck in his throat.

She watched him with curiosity, her mind not having made the connection yet between the sound and his sudden strange behavior. His eyes went from the blood that was spilling through his shirtfront, to her.

She could see tears in his sad eyes. His mouth continued to work at speaking something.

Then she too saw the blood.

He staggered forward toward her, one hand reaching out. She saw that he had soiled the front of his trousers.

In the time it took her to fully realize that he had been shot, Lamar's life drained away.

# CHAPTER 18

English had fired the fatal shot. He had laid the front blade sight of the Winchester in the center of the fat man's chest and squeezed off a round. The rifle kicked back into the shoulder of English.

The others lay among the rocks where they had been watching the man and woman below.

The Anger brothers delighted in the shooting, socking one another in the shoulders over it. Orley Parson lay with his knees pulled up to his chest, full of cramps. The bang of the Winchester only caused the ears to ring and his head to hurt. Dog wished to hell he was someplace else; what English would do to the woman was something he didn't want any part of.

Her first thought at seeing Lamar dead was that she had been rescued; her sense of relief so great that tears flooded her eyes. Confused, she wheeled her horse left and right searching for her rescuers. She could see no one.

A sharp whistle caused her to look up from where she reined the walker in circles. Staring down at her from a stack of big rocks was a swarthy-faced man, a rifle raised in one hand, a battered sombrero pushed back on his head. She could see other men there too, and they did not look like rescuers. The man with the rifle yelled something down to her, she could not understand what he was saying.

He turned toward the others and laughed and then turned back toward her and yelled something again, only this time he grabbed the crotch of his pants and shook it at her.

She drove her heels into the walker's ribs and the horse jumped into a full run, almost unseating her. She knew the big walker could run, she had ridden him full out before. Maybe there was enough of a start to escape these men, to lose them in this devil land. Fear was her ally.

She could feel the walker under her stretching out, the wind pushing back her hair and skirts— taking her breath. She had been so long captured that the first burst of freedom flooded her senses. The pounding of her heart seemed to match that of the animal's hooves.

It seemed as though she had ridden forever, had outrun all the danger, when the accident happened. During a leap, the horse's power gave out from under her. Suddenly she felt the terrible sensation of losing balance, of being thrown free of the saddle and propelled forward, away from the horse. Its magnificent body tumbled head first, hind legs rising in the air, the entire weight of the animal smashing into the ground. And then she felt the impact of her own body hitting the ground. She had only an instant of recognition before the world disappeared.

When she opened her eyes she could make out the blurred image of a swarthy man. She tried bringing her hands up to rub her eyes, but her right shoulder was wracked with pain and she could not lift her arm, her hands were on fire as well.

She saw the man looking at her with curious eyes. She could smell his sweat. There were others there—a couple of men were behind him, grinning down at her from over the leader's shoulder. One man stood soberly watching her; another looked as though he might be sick.

One of the grinning men, a youth with a mustache, leaned over close and grabbed one of her breasts. The dark one kneeling next to her slapped his hand away and growled, "She's mine!"

He undid a blue bandanna from around his neck and wiped her face with it. It stank of sweat. She tried squirming away, but the fire in her shoulder caused her to cry out in pain.

He leaned his face close to hers; his breath was sour. "Do you think you can escape from Englase, eh?" He waited for her to answer and when she did not, he slapped her lightly on the side of the face.

"When do we get a turn with her, English?" It was the one who had grabbed her breast.

English ignored the question. He ordered them to lift her onto his horse. When they moved her the pain in her shoulder felt like fire. He ordered the two young ones to go back and search the bodies of the dead men and bring back anything worth having, including the two horses. Then English mounted behind her on the horse and nudged it into a walk. She saw the two older men mount and follow. Each step the animal took sent stabs of pain through her. She bit her lip to keep from crying out.

They didn't ride long before they stopped again. English lifted her off the horse. Pain shot through her shoulder and down her side; this time she could not hold in the scream.

"You wait here!" He ordered the others. He carried her to a place among tall rocks and laid her down on the ground. The pain was consuming her. He grinned at her anguish as he unbuttoned his pants and knelt before her, pushing her skirts up with his rough hands.

"Don't do this to me!" she ordered through clenched teeth, but she knew she was powerless to stop him.

The others heard her scream. Dog turned and walked away from the rest, hoping he wouldn't have to listen, but still he could hear her. Orley

147

sat on the ground with his knees pulled up to his chest, rocking back and forth with the cramps.

Dog tried to block out the woman's cries of pain by remembering his daughter back in Kansas. She would be younger than this woman but a grown woman by now nonetheless. He wondered what she'd look like grown up but couldn't draw a picture in his mind of anything other than what she'd looked like as a child. The thought of anyone raping his daughter made him grow agitated.

If it were just English, he told himself, he'd risk trying to save the woman—he'd find a way to kill the half-breed and set her free. But there was no way he could take on all of them. Orley Parson would be no trouble, but the Anger brothers. . . . He just could not find the courage to move against them. He leaned against a rock and smoked a cigarette. She stopped screaming after a time.

After English finished with her, each of the two younger ones raped her.

When they finished English and the Anger brothers went through the loot they had stripped from the corpses. Ed came up with a pocket watch and a pinky ring off the body of the man whose skull had been caved in. Earl kept the revolver and gun belt. They each tried on the dead man's boots, but they didn't fit.

They had found nothing worth having on the one English had killed. Then they had discovered the contents of the gunny sacks tied around the sorrel's saddle horn. They sat with the bags open on the ground. Earl raised up two handfuls of paper money to show the Breed.

English snatched the money out of Earl's hands and examined it closely. "Ayiee!"

"Yeah, ain't that about the most sum-a-bitchin' money you ever seen?" cried Ed, digging up two more handfuls. Even Orley had forgotten his miseries for the time being. Money like that would buy a whole lot of relief for a whole long time.

English looked from the bags of money to Dog, who had been standing away from the others.

"You go and have the woman. You, then Orley!" It wasn't a request, it was an order.

"I ain't in no condition for a woman right now," pleaded Orley. "I'm sick as a poisoned coon. Maybe after I get me some medicine, I could do that woman some good, but right now I ain't worth spit."

Dog knew he was being tested and if he refused the offer of the woman, it would be considered a sign of weakness or disloyalty.

"She'd be about your speed there, Dog," said Earl with a smirk. "She ain't much, is she, Ed?"

Ed shook his head stupidly.

Dog had come across a number of men in his lifetime who had rubbed his feelings raw enough

149

to want to kill them on the spot—these were some in front of him now.

"What you wait for, Dog?" English was ready for a fight—it wouldn't take much on Dog's part to provoke it.

"Say, you ain't one of the sissy types that like other men instead of women, are you, Dog?" It was Ed speaking.

Dog knew he had to draw down on them or go to the woman. He ran the odds quickly again through his mind. He turned slowly and started walking in the direction where they had taken her; he could not bring himself to face death.

# CHAPTER 19

Rain the size of nickels awakened Luther Pride. Wet and cold, the rain stung his face and he flung up his arms to protect himself. "Damn! Damn! Damn!" he muttered to himself as he tried to slide farther down into his clothes. The sky boiled up iron-gray clouds with dark underbellies that promised nothing but misery.

He had walked through the night, but near dawn found himself too weary to go on; he had simply lain down on open ground and fallen asleep.

The rain was pushed by a strong northeasterly wind that punished the skin and spirit alike. "Nothing but misery atop of misery," he told himself. Hearing the sound of his own voice was the only comfort he could find for himself.

He grasped his collar and pulled it closed as the rain pelted down on him. A cold rivulet of water ran down the back of his neck and so chilled his skin that he got goose bumps. More water dripped off the tip of his nose. He stood and looked off through the veil of rain.

Slowly he began to walk. His feet felt heavy as

anvils, and at times, the rain fell with such fury he had to force himself not to drop to the ground again. He reached a small rise in the land and in the distance he saw a copse of trees standing like the walls of some ancient, dark castle.

For the three riders, the only decent thing about the rainstorm was that it was at their backs. Nonetheless, at times the rain stung like birdshot.

They spoke little, keeping their heads down, squeezing their eyes shut at times to keep the rain out. The night before had been clear and cool, but the rain had kicked them out of camp before daylight. They hoped it wouldn't last long—it looked as if it would.

Able felt a heavy sense of discouragement. The last half day before, the trail had gone thin; the few tracks found could've been anybody's. As good a tracker as Preacher Billy was, even he admitted that he was relying mostly on instinct and experience in leading them toward the Badlands now. "If you really wanted to get lost from someone, that'd be the place to do it in," he kept saying. Now, with the rain, any further hopes of a trail would be washed away for certain. The only choice seemed to be to keep heading for the Badlands. Able wished there had been more certainty in it.

Hobe rode alongside of Able, he could feel the mood the rain had pressed on all of them.

152

Occasionally he'd look up and see Preacher leaning off to the side of his saddle searching the ground for something that they all knew wasn't going to be there with this rain. The lawman's own sense of frustration was growing. He knew well enough that each passing hour worked against them, worked against Annie being found alive.

It was a hell of a big country and there wasn't a thing that could prevent the men they were after from changing their minds and heading off in any of a thousand new directions. Hobe knew that as well as his own name.

He refused to think of Annie at any given moment—what she might be going through— *if she was still alive.* He'd once helped rescue a mother and daughter who had been kidnapped down in west Texas by Comanches. They had suffered every indignity women could suffer at the hands of men. By the time they had been rescued, they had gone hollow-eyed. The mother babbled like a three-year-old. The girl sat stone-faced and told their rescuers in calm detail every atrocity they had endured. Later, after they were returned home, the daughter climbed out of her bed in the middle of the night, went into her daddy's barn, and hanged herself.

He felt sorry for Annie, for Able. He thought how he'd be feeling if it were his sweetheart they were after right now. His heart ached.

Preacher finally broke the silent procession. He

turned his mule around and walked back to the two trailing men. "I know of an old line shack up near a stand of trees not far from here. It could offer us some shelter from this rain, give it a chance to let up to a reasonable downpour. We cain't make no real progress this-a-way!" he said, extending his arm outwards.

Able wanted to say to hell with stopping, but all they were accomplishing right now was getting soaked and wearing themselves and the animals down. If he had been alone, he would have kept pushing on. And he knew they'd keep going if he said he wanted to, but Preacher was right.

"I guess we can't go on in this rain," said Able. "Most likely if we ain't moving on account of this, they ain't moving."

"Hobe, you agree?" asked Preacher.

"Seems best," said the lawman.

Preacher Bill turned his mule back again and kicked it into a trot—why stay wetter longer?

As Luther Pride drew nearer the stand of woods, he could make out the shape of a building near its edge. His spirit grew brighter at the prospect of shelter—unoccupied shelter. He broke into a gimpy trot toward the building. His steps sloshed against the wet ground.

He slipped and fell down, got up and started running again; he could feel warmth climbing back into his limbs as he ran.

His hand reached the latch of the door and he shook it open and lurched inside, and suddenly the rain wasn't falling on him anymore. His eyes searched the dimness of the one-room building. It was nothing more than a line shack, but it might just as well have been the Palace in San Francisco for all the gladness he found in it. The roof leaked in spots; there was a broken-down cot in one corner, and a three-legged table that had tipped over onto its side. A good ladder-back chair sat as though it were waiting for someone special to show up. All the glass in the windows had been busted out, or nearly so. Yellowed newspaper lined one wall and part of another.

He took off his shirt and squeezed the water out of it and put it back on. He did the same with his pants and socks. It was some better, but not much. He wished to heaven that he had something to start a fire with, but even if he'd had matches, the only thing he could burn would have been the shack.

"The shack lies up in those woods yonder," said Preacher, pointing toward a stand of trees in the distance.

"Whose place is it?" asked Hobe.

"Don't know, it's just always been there as far as I can remember," said Preacher.

Able's gaze took in the entire setup, from woods to shack. There were no animals about, no smoke from the stovepipe sticking through the roof, no woodpile. The place seemed void of trouble. He remembered a tree-lined road in Pennsylvania, it too had seemed safe enough. The ache in his hip was a painful reminder. He felt uneasy. He stood in the stirrups to relieve the pain. He'd just as soon walk rather than ride a horse when his hip got like this.

They rode the horses up into the trees, a small stand of ponderosa pines that smelled sweet in the rain. They slid out of the wet, slick saddles, and hobbled their animals. Hope was, that the rain wouldn't last long. They pulled off their saddles, bedrolls, and saddlebags and carried them toward the shack.

Preacher was in the lead when they started into the cabin, followed by Hobe, with Able bringing up the rear. Preacher had one leg inside the door when he suddenly bounced back off the chest of Hobe Waters, and swore his first words in nearly two years. "Holy hell!" Preacher's boot spur caught on a loose board and he went down in a split like a ballerina. Hobe tried to catch him and wound up dropping all his gear on top of Preacher instead. Able answered the confusion by pulling his pistol and aimed it through the doorway.

Hobe was busy trying to reach through his gear and help Preacher to his feet when Luther Pride came barreling through the door, crashing into all three of them.

• • •

All Luther Pride knew was that one minute he
had been dozing on the floor of the shack,
dreaming of lying on the tiger-skin rug in front
of the fireplace at Big Mamma Cotton's, Dahlia
Rose next to him. And then he heard that shack
door being rattled open and he was staring
directly up into a white man's face standing there
in the doorway. There wasn't but one way out of
that shack and that was through the doorway
where the white man stood. It was some surprise
to go crashing into a whole pack of white men.

Hobe was bowled over backward into Able, whose
gun hand was knocked skyward, blowing a hole
in the rain.

Preacher Bill's head got knocked into the side
of the doorframe by one of Luther's big knees
and that stunned him properly. Hobe found himself slammed down into the mud under the weight
of the black man, who felt as heavy as a stack of
lumber on him. And Luther felt as tangled as a
fish in a net and about twice as determined to get
uncaught. His arms, hands, and legs scrambled to
get free until the moment he felt the cold press
of Able's pistol against his forehead.

"Mister, I don't know who you are, or where
you hope to be, but if you don't want rain to be
the last thing you experience, you'll stay as polite
as a parson."

# CHAPTER 20

"Damn it, Able, let him up, I'm being crushed down here!" It was Hobe struggling to free himself under the weight of the black man.

"Go on, raise up slow," ordered Able, keeping the barrel of his Colt pressed to the dark, wet skin of the man's forehead.

In his panic, Luther had completely forgotten his own weapon; he didn't have any choice but to do as ordered.

After the black man climbed off, Hobe unstuck himself from the muddy ground and wiped his hands against his legs and combed his fingers through his hair in order to dislodge clots of mud. Preacher Billy, still sprawled in the doorway, was trying to shake sense back into his addled brain, his eyeglasses knocked half off and hanging by one ear.

Hobe was still scraping mud off when he took his first full look at the black man. "Son of a bitch! It's Luther Pride! We got him, Able!"

Without realizing it, Able thumbed back the Colt's hammer—the click was audible.

"Don't kill him, Able." It was Preacher, his

voice pinched with the effort of getting to his feet; he clung to the doorway to steady himself. Able realized then how close he had come to killing the man. He had to bite down his anger and take off the pressure his finger was bearing on the trigger. He eased the hammer back down on the pistol.

Hobe ducked inside the cabin and back out again. "She ain't in there," he said. "Where the hell is she?" he asked, putting his face close to that of the black man's.

"Let's take it inside, boys," said Preacher. "We ain't going to settle this any quicker standing out here in the rain." He limped in first, followed by the others.

Preacher found the chair and sat down, something bad was torn up in his knee. They stood there, water dripping off them and gathering in dark puddles at their feet.

"You got about half a minute to tell us what you did with her." Able's words were as cold as his stare.

Luther did not know this man holding the gun on him, but he had known men like him, men with unflinching eyes and words as hard as steel and wills to match. He knew the other two slightly: the squatty marshal and the preacher man. He'd never had any trouble with either, but that didn't mean he wasn't about to; they were white men in a lather.

He returned the gaze of the man who held a pistol to his head. "I didn't do nothing with Miss Annie, it wasn't me who stole her in the first place, but I knowed people would see it that way."

"Hell, this ain't no time to be fooling with us," said Hobe, feeling his own impatience growing. "You come clean now and I'll make sure you get a legitimate trial, you hear me?"

Without turning his head, Luther moved his eyes from the one called Able to stare into the eyes of the lawman. "Mister, I ain't fooling with you. It wasn't me that took the woman, it was her brother and two other men."

Preacher spoke from where he was sitting. "You know me, don't you, Luther?" Luther looked at the bespectacled man for a moment and nodded his head. "Well, I know we ain't never broke bread together, and you ain't never attended my services on Sundays, but I want you to know that we're not going to harm you. You have my word as a Christian man on that. Trouble we got here is that there's one poor soul dead already, and another missing, and every hour that passes just makes everyone's nerves get a little rawer. You got to help us out on this, Luther."

"It was Miss Annie's brother," he began. "He come riding up to the homeplace, him and two other men. She and Mr. Ben took them in. . . ." He told them the rest of the story. ". . . The brother's the smart one," he continued. "He worked it out so it'd look like it was me that done it. The other two, they're just mean and stupid. I killed the one—the mean one, that's how I got back this far."

"It makes sense," said Preacher. "There were more than just two sets of tracks the whole time. Where were they headed?" he asked.

"We was in a land got all broken up, sudden-like—looked like the devil's hideout. But I heard the brother say they was heading for Nebraska Territory."

"The Badlands!" interjected Preacher, "I was sure of it."

"It was a bad land for certain," replied Luther.

"How'd you get here?" asked Hobe. "We didn't see any animals tied up outside."

"Walked. When I killed the one called Jim Buck, the horses got killed too. Had to walk."

Able holstered his revolver. "If he's lying, he's good at it," he said. "You don't strike me as a liar, Mr. Pride."

Preacher let out a sigh of relief. Able offered to bring in the rest of the gear that had been dropped outside in the scuffle. They had nothing to build a fire with, and there was nothing but two biscuits left to eat, which they shared.

"You think you can show us just where it was you killed that fellow and the two horses?" asked Able.

161

"I can get you to the dead man."

"How far do you figure it to be?" asked Hobe.

"Don't know for certain," said Luther, "but I walked all the previous noon and all night too, hard as I could, so whatever that would figure out to be, I don't know. I ain't used to walking, I'm a horseman."

Preacher calculated it in his head. He knew it to be about thirty, maybe forty miles to the Badlands. That would make Luther's walk come out about right.

"It'd be three, four hours of good riding," said Preacher. "Maybe less. Trouble is, I don't believe I can sit a mount, my leg feels bummed up good."

"Fortune's turning," said Hobe, who had taken up watch at one of the broken-out windows. "Rain's nearly stopped altogether."

Preacher hobbled over to look for himself. "Boys, I think the Lord finally got with us on this ride," he said and smiled, the light reflecting off his glasses, hiding the twinkle in his eyes.

"Preacher, if you don't mind waiting here, we can let Mr. Pride ride your mule," said Able.

"Don't see's there's any choice in it, much as I hate getting this close and having to stop. I reckon if Luther can get you as far as the Badlands, you should be able to find them fellows from there on out."

"You ever ride a mule?" asked Able.

"Mister, I fought Indians and stole their ponies."

"You'll ride in the lead, then."

Preacher removed his canvas jacket and handed it to Luther. It had a corduroy collar and a felt lining. "It'll help keep the chill off," he said simply. The black man took it and put it on. It was too short in the sleeves, and the middle was hard to button, but it felt like good news.

"Me and that mule will get along just fine," said Luther. "The coat will be a comfort, sure enough!"

Hobe and Able shook hands with Preacher Billy, left him a canteen of water, and promised to pick him up on the way back through, or see to it someone else did if they came across a homestead first. "I got the Good Book to keep me company," he said, reaching into his saddlebags and pulling out his Bible.

They started out the door. "Able," called Preacher. "I suspect you'll do the right thing given the chance." The two men looked at one another. Able knew full well what Preacher was referring to.

"Preacher, if we get Annie back alive, it will be enough for me."

It was near noon when they stepped out of the shack. The air was filled with mist, but the rain had quit and that was relief enough. Preacher watched them trail out the door and felt badly about seeing them go.

Able was eager to begin. Now that he knew

more of the circumstances of Annie's kidnapping, he was somewhat relieved in feeling certain that no matter what, her own brother wouldn't let harm come to her.

Luther Pride had mixed emotions about the journey. As long as he was mixed up with white men, no matter what the cause, he was bound to see more trouble. And yet, it was hard not to want to help one of the two white people who had befriended him. He recalled a lesson his daddy had tried teaching him when he was still a boy tramping alongside the old man whose single-blade plow had turned up fresh dirt clods for him to break up with his own bare feet.

"Boy," his daddy warned, "they is good men and bad. And I have met my share of both. But when it comes to white men, I've yet to come across one that showed a lick of kindness to colored folks. Come the day I do, I reckon I'll lay down this old plow and raise me up milk and honey. Onliest thing I can tell you about white men, boy, is don't trust 'em."

Luther had always remembered that lesson to be true, more or less.

He mounted the mule and felt halfway comfortable again. A mule wasn't any army mount, and his butt didn't feel quite the same as it did sitting on a McClellen, but it was a damn sight better than walking.

"You better have this back." It was the one

called Able. He held out the gun belt and the holster holding the Remington. He reached out and took it as though it were some sort of prize being offered.

"I reckon if you've fought Indians and stole their ponies, you'll know how to use this when the time comes."

"How do you know I won't use it on you?" For the first time since their encounter, he saw the jaw muscles of the white man relax.

Able half smiled and said, "I'm guessing there are two reasons why you won't use that big iron on me."

"What might they be?" asked Luther.

"Well, first off, you don't seem the sort of man that takes killing lightly."

"And the other?"

"You don't seem like the sort that takes dying lightly, either."

Luther strapped on the gun belt and adjusted the placement of the holster on his hip. "All I've been through lately," he replied, "I wouldn't count on it."

# CHAPTER 21

Dog's only choice was to go to her. They had ordered him to rape the woman, and if he refused, he'd have to face them down.

She looked at him approaching the way an animal caught in a leg trap would watch the approach of the trapper. He could see her skirts had been pushed up past her hips. Her legs were scratched and already showing signs of bruising. Her face was dirty and streaked by her tears, one eye was swollen. Her hair was matted and tangled. He tried not to look at her directly, it made him uncomfortable. He felt embarrassed for her, and sorry for her. He felt sorry for himself for having allowed this to happen to her.

He knelt beside her. She shrank away from him.

"Miss," he began to speak in a low, secretive voice. "I ain't intending on hurting you. . . ." His words trailed off. Her stare bore into him. He felt the intense hatred of her gaze.

"Miss, I ain't like those others, and I am sorry as hell that this has had to happen . . . I couldn't stop it, though . . . please, ma'am, you've got to understand what I'm trying to say here."

A sharp pain passed through her shoulder and down her side and in spite of her resolve, she moaned.

His hand reached out and brushed back some of the hair that had spider-webbed across her face. "Miss, I want to help you . . . but I just can't seem to come up with no way to do so. These men are killers, and they'd kill me just as quick as they would anybody if they got the notion that I was a problem for them."

With all the strength she could summon, she reached her good arm out until her hand rested on his. Her eyes had welled with tears. "Please," she whispered.

"Please, kill me."

He choked down his emotions. His hand reached for the butt of his pistol. It would be easy to slide it out of the holster, put it to her temple and pull the trigger. He would have done it for a wounded animal, a suffering horse. At least he'd be doing something for her. But his sense of shame at what he had already allowed to happen to her would not allow him to kill her.

He had made up his mind. "Miss, I want you to listen to me. I'm going to help you. You've got to trust me, though. If we get caught, then we'll both die, that's a certainty." She steadied herself and looked at him through wet eyes. He could see a change in them.

"How much are you hurt?" he asked. "Could you get up and walk if you had to?"

She struggled to regain her voice. "I . . . my shoulder . . . I think it's broken."

He bent over her and examined it. The top of her dress had been torn away, but she had managed to replace it loosely with her good hand. He gently removed it enough to see the damage to her shoulder.

It was badly distorted at the joint; the shoulder blade rode high and out of place. It was dislocated, not broken. He wasn't any doctor, but he'd seen enough cowboys and bronco riders thrown to the ground with shoulders just like this one. He'd popped some back in place, too. He knew how much it hurt, popping a shoulder back in; he'd done it to a range partner once and the man had screamed clear across Kansas, but was up riding and working the next day.

After examining the shoulder he leaned back on his heels and looked at her. "Your shoulder ain't broke, miss—that's the good news. The bad news is, popping it back in place is going to hurt like hell. You feel you can handle any more than what you've been through already?"

She bit down on her lower lip and nodded that she could. He took a bandanna from his back pocket and tied it around her mouth. "It'll help quiet you in case you have to scream out," he told her as he knotted it at the back of her head. He knew she would scream; he didn't want the others to hear her, though, and come look.

"You ready now, miss?"

She closed her eyes as he lifted her up into a sitting position. He placed his hands in position, one in the front, the other behind the damaged shoulder. He leaned near her and whispered, "Hold on!" When he snapped the shoulder she let out one short cry and fainted from the pain. He had failed to pop it back in the first try, but with a second effort, with her unconscious and her muscles relaxed, he was easily able to snap the joint into place. He used his knife to cut the sleeves off his own shirt, knotted the ends together, and made a sling with which to bind her shoulder and arm so she wouldn't have a tendency to move it once she came to. At least that part of her would heal.

He laid her back down gently and sat beside her. He wasn't at all sure how he was going to help her escape from them. He simply knew that he couldn't allow them to hurt her anymore; if it came to that, he'd kill her first. He figured for right now, she was safe. The others seemed to have had their fill of her for the time being.

The three riders topped a rise and looked down on a stretch of land only one of them had ever seen before.

"That's the place," said Luther. "It's the place

they brung us, the place where I killed one of them."

Able's heart sank; it would be pure luck to find anyone in the puzzle of land that lay before them.

They spurred their mounts forward. "You still think you can find the dead man?" asked Hobe.

"I can find him." He headed the mule toward a far spiraling rock that looked as though it had a knob atop it. "It'd be near the base of that rock yonder. Unless the wolves has carried him off, the fellow I killed would be lying somewhere near that rock."

The man lay frozen in death. The two horses already were bloated to an unnatural size. Insects had begun their feast on man and beast alike. The riders dismounted and took a closer look at the carnage. It was plain that either wolves or coyotes had come to dinner sometime during the night before. The smell was beginning to get bad.

Luther stood back and waited for the two men to examine the scene. "You recognize this one, Hobe?" asked Able.

"Well, he's swelled up some from the heat, and the birds has pecked his eyes out, but I don't recollect ever seeing this one around before. What you say they called him?" asked Hobe, turning back to where Luther was standing.

"Heard them call him Jim Buck."

"Don't recall ever hearing the name either," said Hobe, shaking his head and giving the corpse one last look.

Able turned toward his horse. "It's a good thing Preacher ain't here, he'd want us to take time and bury him."

Hobe noted the edginess in Able's voice. "Which way'd you see the others head off to?" he asked Luther.

Luther pushed his weight up onto the mule and turned the animal down an arroyo. The others followed.

Nearly an hour of wandering brought them to the bodies of two more dead men. "Lord almighty," muttered Luther. "That's the other two that robbed the bank and kidnapped me and Miss Annie. That one there is the one they called Lamar," he said pointing at the massive body lying some twenty yards away from the other corpse. "And this one here is her brother Hap."

Hobe had dismounted and kicked the heavy rock off the face of the smaller man. "His head's caved in to mush," he announced, turning to Able.

Both men got down off their mounts and walked with the lawman over to the body of the big man. "He's been shot in the chest," said Hobe.

"Not only that," said Luther, "but these men's been robbed, too." It was obvious from the way their pockets were turned out and one's boots were missing.

Hobe felt near reluctance at looking any farther for fear he would find the body of Annie lying among the rocks somewhere. Able felt the oppression too. Whoever had killed these men had either killed her as well, or taken her. The obvious truth was that if she was still alive, she was in even more danger than when she was abducted from Deadwood.

"Able, we've got to search around here for her . . . you realize there's every chance she could be . . ." Hobe didn't finish it, he didn't need to.

"I know," was all Able said. "I know."

# CHAPTER 22

He had waited until she came to. She looked as if all the blood had gone out of her; she was the color of rice paper.

"Miss, you passed out, but I got the shoulder back in, it'll heal okay, I believe. I tied it up so's you can't move it around. It'll hurt some for a day or so, but not nearly so bad as before."

She listened to him speak, barely able to concentrate on what he was telling her. "Do you have water?" she whispered. She could see by his expression he hadn't any. He shook his head slightly and said there was some back at the camp.

"I'm going to help you back. You remember that I asked you to trust me, that I was going to help you?" He waited for her to answer. She simply looked at him with eyes that spoke of too much pain.

"Well, miss, I'm still asking you to trust me. The onliest chance we've got is to get mounted. And the only way we're going to do that is to get back to camp and hope to hell we can sneak out on a horse when they're not watching." He paused long enough to see if she had a reaction to anything he was saying.

"It ain't much of a plan, but it's all I can come up with. I could try killing some of them, but it's not likely I could kill all of them before they gunned me down." He drew a deep breath and looked at her for a long, hard moment. "It's just that . . . I'm afraid. . . ." He didn't finish the thought.

She understood his fear. In spite of everything that had happened, she found herself still afraid of dying. There were, however, moments of hopelessness when she welcomed death. But every time there was the slightest bit of hope, she wanted desperately to live.

"Help me to sit up," she asked him.

He braced one arm under her and lifted her to a sitting position. The terrible throbbing in her shoulder was absent; she was able to take a deep breath and gather some strength.

"What is your name?" she asked him.

He felt ashamed to tell her. She waited for him to answer. Finally he said, "Bishop. Wynn Bishop, miss."

"My name is Annie Matters," she told him. "You are a good man, Mr. Bishop."

"Not so good to be riding with the likes of them," he answered, nodding his head back toward where the others were camped.

"We all make mistakes, Mr. Bishop."

He fell silent.

"You feel up to going back?" he asked finally.

"I'd rather not have to," she said. "But I'll do what you say."

He helped her to her feet. She felt unsteady and leaned her weight against him. He encircled her waist with one arm.

"Promise me something, Mr. Bishop," she said, trying to gain her balance.

"What's that, miss?"

"Promise me that no matter what, you won't let them rape me again. If we can't find a way to escape, promise me you'll kill me if they come at me again."

He did not answer her.

"Promise me, Mr. Bishop. Please!"

"I promise, Annie. I promise."

Dog saw them gathered in a circle sitting on their haunches as he and the woman approached the camp. They were too busy counting out the money into stacks to notice him walking up with her. He took her to where he had placed his bedroll before, and eased her down.

They were gathered around the money, counting it out into stacks. English had Orley count it out because English did not know reading, writing, or ciphering. Orley was having a hard time concentrating; his hands shook as he counted out the paper money and stacked it, putting a fist-sized rock atop each stack to keep it from blowing away. The Anger brothers watched him like hawks.

English squatted there, stoic, as though what was taking place meant nothing to him. But he had already made up his mind that he alone would leave the camp; maybe he would take the woman as well. He no longer had any need of the others. He simply needed the right moment to kill them. The Anger brothers would have to be killed first, they were the true danger—Orley Parson would be as easy as killing a chicken.

But English wasn't the only one doing some thinking. In spite of the tremors and the cramps, Orley Parson had decided it would be a damn shame for such a fortune to be wasted on men who would squander it on whores and whiskey and horses. Whereas, someone like himself could find more refined uses for this money: French cuisine in San Francisco, the opera, tailor-made suits. But mostly, Orley envisioned the lure of the opium dens, the tranquillity that so much money could buy him.

Meanwhile, Dog eyed the horses, which were still saddled, their reins tied around heavy rocks to keep them from wandering off. He wondered if the woman could ride. He was about to ask her when he heard the Anger brothers order, "Throw up your goddamn hands!"

English and Orley Parson found themselves

staring down the black mouths of old navy Colt pistols that weren't held all that steadily in the hands of the two former Ohio farm boys.

Ed turned just enough to wiggle the barrel of his pistol toward Dog. "You better git over here," he said, his voice high and thin with excitement. Dog whispered to the woman to remain still and not move as he slowly stood.

"Son, you'll get no quarrel from me," he told Ed, showing the palms of his hands. He knew that right now, in their state of excitement, they were dangerous as hell. English knew it too. Dog moved over to the others. Earl ordered them to squat down and be quiet while he took their sidearms, or else Ed would cut them to pieces. He patted Orley down for a weapon since none was evident and, finding none, he slapped the shaking man on the back of the head.

"Put all that money back into them totes, you silly old bastard," ordered Ed. Orley did as told, taking double handfuls at a time until the task was complete. He handed the bags up to Earl.

The two brothers stepped back, Ed with a pistol in each hand pointing it down at the heads of the squatting men. Earl held the money bags. They both felt pretty amazed at how easy it had been to rob these hardcases.

"We could kill you, you know?" said Earl, feeling brassy. "You give us any trouble and we still might."

177

English chewed hard on the inside of his mouth. To be robbed by two gringo pups was an insult. He spat in the dust and narrowed his eyes at them. "Maybe you will be the one to get killed, eh?" He curled his lips up into a mocking smile.

"Why, you bean-eatin' son of a bitch!" Ed yelled, pushing the barrel of one of the navy Colts he held into the hollow of English's cheek. "I'll blow your goddamn head off right here."

Earl had dropped one of the sacks on the ground and pulled one of the captured pistols out of his belt and waved it in the faces of Dog and Orley. "Hell, maybe we ought to just kill them all and be done with it here and now," he whooped.

Between having the sweats and shakes, and the way the Anger brothers were threatening to kill them all, Orley Parson felt like he was going to come right out of his skin.

"I can't abide the thought that you boys mean any harm to me," he cried. "I've never borne you anything but goodwill. You take me with you and I'll guide you to better times than you've ever known before. I've got the words of the spirits in me—I know things other men don't!"

"Quiet that old son of a bitch down, Ed," ordered Earl, who had taken the bags of money over to one of the horses and was tying them around the saddle horn.

Ed brought the barrel of his pistol down across

Orley Parson's shiny head with a smacking thud that split open the man's scalp and knocked him cold. And as though he had made a mistake by hitting him, Ed took a step back, looked down at the comatose man and fired a shot into his chest; the bullet smacked home, dead center.

Instantly Dog knew that they would all be killed now that the bloodletting had started. Instinctively, he made a desperate bid. He scooped up handfuls of dirt and flung them into Ed's face, and simultaneously barreled into the half-blinded man's midsection, grasping for the gun. English dove behind the cover of Orley's body as Earl fired off two wild shots in their direction. One bit into the dead man's leg, the other kicked up dirt thirty yards beyond.

Dog yanked the gun from Ed's hand and clubbed him hard across the face with it, dropping him to his knees. And as Ed fell, stunned from the first blow, Dog smashed a second blow to the side of his head, knocking him over onto his side.

Earl's pistol barked again. Dog felt something kick him in the heel. He glanced down at his foot. The bullet had torn off the heel of his left boot. Immediately, he turned, brought up the pistol he had taken from Ed, and aimed it at Earl, who was desperately trying to shoot his pistol and hold onto the reins of his skittish horse at the same time.

Dog squeezed off a shot that should have hit its target but missed.

Earl heard the bullet whistle past his head. He scrambled onto the mount he had been holding and practically kicked in its sides in his effort to escape.

Dog knew there wasn't a chance in hell of hitting the fleeing man, but his frustration made him pull the trigger anyway. He saw the flop-brim hat of the rider go whizzing off his head, and then horse and rider disappeared beyond a stand of rocks.

The gunplay had spooked the other horses and they had scattered off some distance. English was already running after them. Annie had remained where Dog had ordered her to—out of harm's way.

Dog moved to her in a hurry, it was the chance they needed. He reached down and lifted her up. "We've got to run for it, Annie—we won't have no other chances!" She looked at him but did not move.

He glanced over his shoulder. English was still chasing after the horses that had stopped in a small bunch several hundred yards away. It wouldn't take him long to catch one of them.

"Miss, we've got no time to waste. Once he catches one of them horses, he'll have a gun. There are rifles strapped on the saddles. You understand me?"

She seemed not to hear him.

He suspected that it was fear that froze her. He checked the chambers of the revolver in his hand—three shells left. He turned back again to check English's progress—he had come to within fifty yards of the horses. He had slowed to a walk so as not to spook them any further.

Dog turned to the woman again and slapped her hard across the face. She looked at him with hurt and anger. "Good!" he said. "At least you're back in this world. Now let's go!"

# CHAPTER 23

Earl Anger bashed in the flanks of the piebald mare with his boot heels as he leaned over the mare's neck, the rough mane whipping at his face. In seconds, he was clean out of sight of the camp, the mare's hooves chewing up ground.

He did not know exactly how far he had ridden before he reined in the mare. Her chest and fore-legs were lathered and she was blowing air. Earl chided himself for leaving his brother back there—it was a sad and pitiful sight to see his own flesh and blood being beaten like that. Sitting there thinking on it got him feeling sad and mad.

"What the hell am I goin' to do?" he asked himself aloud. "Just what the hell am I goin' to do?" He felt the need to relieve himself. He dismounted and held the reins of the horse in one hand while he fumbled with the buttons on his pants with the other. He went against a rock and felt better.

He walked in circles trying to figure out exactly what he should do. He paused and checked the knots on the money bags, making sure they were secure. One minute, he felt brave and wanted to go back for Ed; the next, he wanted to scramble back onto the mare and ride as far away as she could carry him.

He talked to himself about how he should just ride on back and kill English and Dog—especially Dog, for whipping Ed. But all of them, even the woman, deserved to taste his bullets. Then it occurred to him that English would be coming after *him,* ready to chase him to hell and back if need be. He imagined what English would do to him if he caught him. His imagination caused him to hurry to his mount.

He threw himself in the saddle and spurred the mare into a gallop: *To hell with it! This was one of them times when brother Ed was going to have to fend for himself!* Earl had pretty much convinced himself that if things were reversed, Ed would've done the same.


English approached the horses slowly, talking to them in Spanish, murmuring soft words as though they were senoritas at a dance. They eyed him cautiously. He closed in on the one that seemed less suspicious about his approach—a chestnut gelding—Dog's horse.

He tried remembering what Dog called his animal. He clucked his tongue softly. He got within a few steps of the animal and started to reach for the dangling reins. The gelding raised its head and danced sideways a few steps. English cursed its contrariness under his breath, then the name came to him: Sandy.

"Sandy, you come, eh." The gelding pricked up its ears. "Ah, si, you come, I take good care of you." He held steady as he came closer. His hand touched the reins and the animal was his. He stroked its neck as he moved around the other side and swung himself up into the saddle. His mind raced as to who he should go after first: Dog and the woman, or the gringo pup who had taken his money and tried to kill him.

His hand snaked the Winchester from the saddle scabbard. He cranked the lever and jacked a shell into the chamber.

Ed Anger was trying desperately to rise from the fog and pain of being pistol whipped. His skull felt as if it had been kicked into pieces. Blood pooled thick in his hair and oozed from a wide gash high on the side of his cheek from the two blows Dog had delivered. He had trouble focusing his vision as he struggled first to his knees, and then to his feet.

He cried out once for his brother, *"Ea-rrl!"* His vision cleared just enough to see a blur of a horse and rider bearing down on him. He was relieved that his brother had not abandoned him.

Ed's relief turned to terror when he realized the horseman was not Earl. He tried to run but the chest of the horse was soon so close he could reach out and touch it. The full weight of the animal caught him head-on, knocking him to the ground with such force that all the air rushed out of his lungs. The hooves of the animal struck him across the neck and shoulder, and broke one of his ankles.

He tried rolling over on his belly when he heard the horse come on again. He was fighting for his wind and everything was a sheet of pain pulled over him.

The horse ran over him again, this time kicking him in the head and once in the back. He curled up from the pain and screamed with what little breath he had in him. He lay there for what seemed like a long time. Waiting. He didn't know if he could move. He spat dust and blood from his mouth and tried to clear his eyes with the back of one hand.

And then he felt something hard and small at the back of his head—something pushing down.

"Roll over, gringo, so I can have a look at your ugly face!"

The thing lifted from the back of his head and he rolled over. The hard, small weight of the barrel end of a Winchester was pressed against his forehead.

"You the one gonna blow my goddamn head off, eh!" English pressed the end of the barrel harder against Ed's forehead. "You think you are some badman or something!"

The bullet hammered death into the brain of Ed Anger. As a gesture, English pulled a dirk from inside his boot and cut the dead man's throat.

Dog heard the crack of the Winchester echo through the rocks where he and the woman were working their way. She was having difficulty keeping the pace he had wanted to maintain; even the fear of being caught and killed by English could not hasten her steps. The shot told Dog that English had caught a horse. He could only suppose that English had just killed Ed Anger. He and the woman would be next, then English would go after Earl.

They had heard a shot in the distance. Faint, but nonetheless real. But which way? They looked toward one another for the answer.

"I think it came from over there!" yelled Hobe, pointing to the east of where they were.

"I think more toward the south," said Luther.

"I tend to agree with you," said Able, shaking his head. "But out here, and at such a distance, it's damn hard to tell."

They waited in silence for a moment, hoping to hear another shot.

"Well, let's fan out if we have to, there's no

time to waste!" shouted Able, spurring his horse in the direction he and Luther believed the shot had come from. Hobe was about to head in the other direction when the rider came crashing up through an arroyo and directly in front of them.

The horseman rode the piebald right into the midst of three men aiming their pistols at him. He jerked back so hard on the reins, the mare nearly sat down in a sliding stop.

Dust from the horse's slide roiled up around them and then cleared. Luther recognized the sacks tied to the man's saddle horn as those Hap Patterson had used to put the bank's stolen money in.

"What's in them bags, mister?" Luther asked the rider.

"What the hell business is that of yours, you black son of a bitch!"

Luther cocked back the hammer on the big Remington.

"You're in an awful ugly position to be calling names," said Able. "This man asked you a question, we're all waiting for an answer."

Earl's face turned the color of buttermilk. "Took 'em off some no-good sum-a-bitch that killed my brother and tried doing the same to me," he lied. "I shot him in the goddamn neck's what I did."

Hobe dismounted, walked to the mounted man, undid the sacks and opened them up. "It's money, lots of it," he said peering down into the sacks.

"Where'd you leave this fellow you shot in the neck?" asked Able, his suspicions heavy.

"Hell, I don't know—back there somewheres," he answered, tossing his head.

"That man you shot, he have a woman with him?" asked Hobe.

Earl studied hard in his mind whether to answer that there was or there wasn't. He needed to get shed of these men before English caught up with him.

"Ye—yes! He had a woman with him. He had a woman and another man and they killed my brother. Tried to kill me, too, but I got away and took their goddamn money!"

In an instant, Able had dismounted, crossed the space between them, and jerked the rider from his horse.

"Which way? Where?" He had a fistful of the man's collar knotted up in his hand. Earl's eyes bugged out and sweat ran down into them until it felt like pins were poking into them.

"Th—there, back there," he said, pointing in the direction that Luther and Able had believed they heard the lone shot come from.

All the anger in Able's body unleashed itself in a vicious right hand that swung up from the waist and landed flush on the side of Earl's chin. The blow broke his jaw and sent a white-hot pain through his face. His knees buckled and he slumped down in the dirt and cradled his face in both hands.

"Mr. Pride, I'd be obliged if you would stay here and guard this horse apple. I can trust you to use your own judgment as to his treatment."

Luther smiled. *It sure was good to see white men knocking hell out of one another for a change.*

"But if he kicks up any fuss," Able added, "I'd be just as obliged if you were to shoot him."

"It'd be all my pleasure, Mr. Guthrie."

# CHAPTER 24

Dog could hear English in the rocks below where he and the woman had taken refuge. Bold as brass, the Breed was calling to them. "Okay, Dog, you come on out now and I'll let you live. You hear me, Dog? You don't come out, I have to kill you."

Dog checked the chambers of the pistol again. Three shells—he would have to make each one count when the time came.

"Come on down, Dog, I let you go—hell, I got no-ting against you. You give me the woman, okay, I still let you go."

Dog assessed their surroundings. They had worked themselves up against a stand of rocks that offered no further retreat. He looked at the woman beside him. Even if they could run, she didn't appear to have anything left. He thought about his daughter and ached for the chance to see her.

He leaned over and whispered in Annie's ear. "Miss, me and you together don't stand a tinker's chance—English will find us if we just sit here, and there ain't no real place to run." He paused long enough to look at the pistol in his hand. "All we got are three chances to come out of this thing." She acknowledged with a nod of her head.

"The way I figure it is, you've been through nearly all the hell you can stand. And I've done all the living I need to, if it comes to that. But I ain't quite ready to give up just yet." His manner brought her renewed strength.

"Miss, I'm going to try and work my way around to where he's at—all I need is one good shot. But I can't carry you with me and do it. I need you to stay put. And you got to keep quiet, no matter what. You understand me?" He took her hand and squeezed it gently. She understood.

"Good," he said to her. "Now remember, Annie, not a peep."

Keeping bent at the waist, he moved to his right—as near as he could tell from where English was calling—he would be circling to the half-breed's left.

English sensed he was closing in on them; he could see from the lay of the land, there weren't a hell of a lot of places they could go, or hide. He would take pleasure in killing both of them.

"Dog," he continued to call, "you come on now, you and the woman—we all go after the money together. What you think of that, eh?"

He walked the horse between rocks in a back-

and-forth manner as though he were searching out stray cattle.

Dog circled among the rocks and was closing the distance between English and him. He stepped behind a large boulder and when the Breed called out to them again, Dog knew he was within firing distance. English had to be just the other side of the rock.

He took a deep breath and stepped around the rock, bringing the revolver up at arm's length ready to fire.

All that lay within the front sight of the pistol was his own horse, standing as though it had been waiting for him. Dog had barely time to comprehend when he heard English laugh behind him.

"You better not turn around, Dog. You won't like what I have waiting for you. Where you leave the woman, eh? You better tell me—I find her anyway, sooner or later?"

"Go to hell!" yelled Dog as he spun around in a last effort to stop English.

The Winchester exploded, the bullet shattering Dog's spine. His legs went numb and he fell instantly. A fire spread throughout his chest, and it felt like all the air was going out of him.

English's shadow fell across him. "You're one dead bastard, Dog," he said. "You tell me where the woman is, I'll keel you quick—you won't have to suffer no more, eh?"

"You're a half-mix son of a bitch," answered Dog through clenched teeth. "Your mother's a Durango whore!"

English brought the Winchester up from where he had been holding it at his side. He pumped three slugs into Dog's face, blowing out the back of his head.

Able and Hobe heard the rifle shots splitting the air. They sounded as if they had been fired right in front of them. The two men pulled their pistols and moved forward.

English performed one final gesture of hatred toward the dead man by urinating on him. When he finished, he turned to where the horse stood, its reins weighted down by a large rock. He swung up in the saddle and sat there for a moment, letting his senses tell him where the woman was hiding. He sniffed the air, trying to smell her, smell her fear. He walked the horse off nearly in a direct line to where she sat hunched, her skirts tenting her legs and feet, her hands cupping her ears.

English sang something in Spanish, something she could hear but could not understand.

As he approached her, she screamed. A long, high wail split the air with a sound that seemed incapable of coming from a human.

Able and Hobe heard it too, just as they saw the

back of a horseman riding nonchalantly toward a row of tumbled boulders.

Hobe Waters fired off a shot that struck the rump of the man's horse and caused it to leap and jolt sideways, nearly tossing the rider to the ground.

The horseman regained his balance and wheeled around in time to see the two men below him.

Able wasted no time in firing the second shot. The bullet from the .41 caliber hit the man's left leg. Hobe fired twice more in quick succession, his bullets hitting the man's horse and pitching it sideways. The rider was barely able to leap free.

Despite the onslaught, the horseman came up firing the Winchester, the first shot searing a line across the top of Able's shoulder as though it had been burned with a branding iron. The second shot caught Hobe just above the buckle of his belt and tore him from the saddle.

Able jumped free of his mount as the horseman jacked another shell in the chamber of his rifle and drew aim. The two men were not more than forty paces apart.

The horseman fired first, his shot went wild. He levered the Winchester again but this time the firing pin fell on an empty chamber. The snap seemed small.

Able walked in a steady straight line toward him, his gun hand held straight out, the barrel never wavering from its target. Able's bullet took

English dead center and knocked him over on his back. Able continued to walk toward the man and pulled the trigger again and again.

Able found her hiding among the rocks. She looked at him with disbelieving eyes. He held her for a long time before carrying her down to where Hobe lay wounded.

"You're safe now, Annie," Able told her. "It's over."

He went over to Hobe. The lawman's breathing was labored, his eyes recognized little, not even the face of a friend. Able tried to lift the dying man, but Hobe moaned from somewhere down deep and Able knew the pain of such effort was too consuming. He removed a saddle from one of the horses and placed it under the wounded man's head and drew a blanket over him—there was little else he could do except sit with him.

Annie sat staring at the dying Hobe Waters. She had seen too many men die, and yet she could not take her eyes from him.

The sound of riders coming caused Able to reach for the Winchester. He moved in front of her, rifle raised to his shoulder.

"Whoa in there," called the voice of Luther Pride.

Able gestured, relieved. "Ride in," he called back.

The black man walked his horse in, trailing the

horse of Earl Anger, who rode with his wrists bound and a rope around his neck.

"I heard the shooting and decided to come see—but it looks like I'm too late." The black man saw the wounded lawman lying near where Annie sat.

She looked up to see Earl Anger watching her. She pushed herself from the ground and ran to where Able was standing. Before he could stop her, she drew the pistol from his holster. The explosion shattered the air.

"You bastard!" she screamed as she tried desperately to cock back the hammer again. Her first shot had barely missed Earl Anger's cheek.

Able grabbed her hand before she could fire again. "Don't do it, Annie—" He took the pistol from her.

She looked into Able's eyes and he could see all the hurt gathered there. "It's over," he said. "Annie, you're going to be all right. Nobody's going to hurt you again."

That night Able went back and forth between the two dearest people in his life. Annie slept the fitful sleep of nightmares—jolting awake, her eyes wild with fright, her body shaking until he could calm her again. Hobe barely moved and nothing they did could stop the slow leak of blood from his chest wound.

Luther Pride sat up with Able and helped him tend to Hobe Waters.

"He seemed a fair man, what little I knew of him," said Luther at one point during the long night.

Able had to bite back his own anger and sorrow.

"He was a good man," said Able. "I never knew him to take advantage of another man and he always stuck in a fight."

Sometime in the night, with all the silence surrounding them, Hobe Waters slipped into the unknown. Able wrapped the blanket around him and held his hand for a long time. He let the memories come back—the high times, and the low, the two had shared. Dying must be hard, he thought, but maybe not as hard as being left behind to grieve. In the morning he and Luther dug a grave and marked it with a pile of rocks. It was all Able could do, the last act of friendship for Hobe.

He awakened Annie and washed her face with canteen water and made her drink some. He put the blanket she had been sleeping on around her shoulders and held her for a while.

After a time she spoke to him.

"Able, I'm sorry about Hobe."

He tried to hush her. "Don't fret anymore, Annie. This will all pass."

"I want you to bury that man over there," she said, pointing to the body of Dog. "He tried to save me, he wasn't like the others. He didn't . . ."

"I'll take care of it."

Able and Luther placed rocks over the body of Dog. "What about those others?" asked Luther, looking at the bodies of Ed Anger, Orley Parson, and English.

"Let the wolves have their supper—I've no more time to waste on them," said Able.

The black man shrugged. "That's fine with me. We ought to be leaving soon, though," he said looking up at the sky. "I wouldn't care to spend another night in these Badlands—leastways, not with all this death about."

Luther and the prisoner, Earl Anger, mounted up.

Able returned to Annie. Her gaze met his.

"I'll be all right, Able. It won't ever be the same again, but I'll be all right."

He put her on his horse and mounted up behind her.

"We'll ride together for a while," he said trailing the reins of Hobe's horse. She felt the security of his strong arms around her as they headed back to Deadwood after they stopped to pick up Preacher Billy.

**Center Point Large Print**
600 Brooks Road / PO Box 1
Thorndike ME 04986-0001 USA

(207) 568-3717

US & Canada:
1 800 929-9108
www.centerpointlargeprint.com